Pleasures and Days

Pleasures and Days

Marcel Proust

Translated by Andrew Brown

ET REMOTISSIMA PROPE

Hesperus Classics

Hesperus Classics
Published by Hesperus Press Limited
4 Rickett Street, London sw6 1ru
www.hesperuspress.com

Pleasures and Days first published in French as *Les Plaisirs et les Jours* in 1896
This translation first published by Hesperus Press Limited, 2004

Introduction and English language translation © Andrew Brown, 2004
Foreword © A.N. Wilson, 2004

Designed and typeset by Fraser Muggeridge
Printed in Italy by Graphic Studio Srl

isbn: 1-84391-090-x

CONTENTS

Marcel Proust had completed the stories, poems and fragments in this volume before he was twenty-two years old. He wrote them in the intervals of being a bored and unwilling law student who would rather read Ruskin than jurisprudence, and who, rather than revise for exams, would prefer to cultivate artists and *grandes dames*. Indifferent to his legal studies, he pursued his social life with the dedication of an academic anthropologist or natural historian. Just as the youthful Darwin had painstakingly observed the minute gradations of finches' beaks in the Galapagos islands – an observation which would eventually turn into the most earth-changing scientific theory ever propounded – so the young Proust, noting how a certain social species might turn up now in a great salon, now in an artist's studio, and again in a low dive – had begun the process of accumulating knowledge which would produce the greatest masterpiece of French fiction: *In Search of Lost Time*.

What will immediately strike any reader of this volume of short stories is how surely, and from the first, Proust knew his theme. The death of the eponymous hero in the first story is so – what other word can one use? – Proustian. As the young nobleman lies back on the pillows, there comes to him on the evening air the sound of a church bell from a distant village, and it brings to him the involuntary recollection of those times, during childhood, when his mother came to kiss him goodnight, slipping into his bedroom before she herself retired to sleep, and how, knowing that he was restless, she would warm his feet with her hands. If not actually the experience of the narrator of *In Search of Lost Time*, such a memory, at such a moment, reverberates with Proustian association. So, also, do at least two other of the story's leitmotivs, the Platonic adoration felt by the Viscount for the Duchess, which seems to foreshadow young Marcel's love for the Duchesse de Guermantes; and – much more vividly – the theme of the foreseen death, intruding itself into the trivial calendars of human appointments and diversions.

The little boy, Alexis, in this early story, is given a horse each year for his birthday. If his uncle is truly mortally ill, will he live long enough to give the youth the promised carriage to go with these horses on his sixteenth birthday? A signal comes, on Alexis's fourteenth birthday, that the uncle's death is near, since he offers him a carriage as well as a second horse. The boy knows that the man is thinking, 'as otherwise you'd risk never having the carriage at all'.

The question of whether the Duchess of Bohemia will or will not attend a ball after his death, or whether she will stay away as a mark of mourning and respect, looms larger in the young Viscount's mind than mortality itself. All this tragicomedy is of a piece with the man who would one day write that scene about the Duchesse de Guermantes's red shoes, which is not merely one of the high points of the novel, but also, arguably, one of the greatest scenes ever devised by any writer. In the juvenile scene, the callousness of the Duchesse is of a Firbankian brittleness: 'nothing would ever console me, in all eternity,' not because of her admirer's death, but 'if I didn't go to that ball'.

One of the recurrent themes in this volume is Proust's empathy with Van Dyck, 'prince of tranquil gestures', about whom he wrote a poem. 'You triumph [...] / In all the lovely things that will soon die'. He sees in the seventeenth-century Court painter the model of the type of artist he will himself become. Just as Van Dyck immortalised the generation who were defeated in the English Civil War, so Proust's Long Gallery of canvas holds in immortal imagination the transitory lives of those whose way of life – and, in many cases, actual existence – was eliminated by the First World War.

Perhaps the Van Dyck poem reflects elements of Proust's friendship with Jacques-Emile Blanche, then a young painter and a keen frequenter, like Proust himself, of the *salons* of the rich and fashionable. Blanche was a much less skilful painter than Proust was a writer, but to visit the gallery at Rouen and see his paintings of the friends he had in common with the novelist is to be visited by a frisson of recognition. If not our old friends in their rounded perfection, here are recognisable sketches for portraits which would on the canvases of the master Proust become Robert de Saint-Loup and Mme Verdurin and the Baron de Charlus.

As in the *Search*, there are recurring characters and themes throughout the volume. Presumably the callous Duchess so beloved of the Viscount in the first story is the same as the country bumpkin Violante in the second. She meets a young Englishman on the hunting field and he despises her simplicity. She discovers how ridiculously easy it is to penetrate 'society' and how empty are the rewards of social success. There both is and isn't irony in Proust's use, as chapter headings, of epigrams from Thomas à Kempis. If he had followed the counsels of *The Imitation of Christ:* 'Be afraid of contact with young or worldly persons. Never have any desire to appear before the great', we should have had no *Search*. Nevertheless, when he reaches the end of his chronicle, Marcel, like a ideal monk, is confined to his cell, and contemplates the lives of the *faubourgs* with the purest *contemptus mundi*.

Purest? No. For the abiding fascination of snobbery – and Proust is Grand High Priest of snobs – is that snobs are not necessarily more trivial than the unworldly. 'Your soul is indeed, in Tolstoy's turn of phrase, a deep dark forest. But the trees in it are of a particular species – they are genealogical trees. People say you're a vain woman? But for you the universe is not empty, but full of armorial bearings.' As Proust observes in his notes 'To a snobbish woman', the dedicated social climber is steeped in history. The new friends acquired by the snob come accompanied by a great gallery of their ancestors' portraiture. In mastering the names of all the aristocrats sitting at her table, the hostess has also learnt the names of the chivalry of France, assembled on medieval battlefields. This perception will mature into one of the central reveries of Proust's masterpiece as he gazes at the Guermantes heraldic stained glass in Combray parish church, watching the sun stream through it onto the wedding guests and illuminate the pimple on the face of his beloved Duchesse.

Proust, as well as being a great storyteller, is also a sage. There are more wise maxims in Proust's pages than in La Rochefoucauld, and as many wise *pensées* as in Pascal. It is remarkable that even in these early stories he had developed this faculty. 'The libertine's desire to take a virgin is still a form of the eternal homage paid by love to innocence.' Or, 'Women incarnate beauty without understanding it.' (Discuss!) Or, 'The abuse of alcohol and women is the very condition of their inspiration, if not of their genius'.

His critical faculties are as sharp in youth as in maturity too: witness the witty exchanges about music in 'Bouvard and Pécuchet on Society and Music'. When one speaker points out that Saint-Saëns lacks content and Massenet form, the tennis ball is very firmly whacked back over the net: 'That's the reason why the one educates us and the other delights us, but without elevating us'.

Proust dedicated his little book to Willie Heath, a young English dandy whom he encountered in the Bois de Boulogne in the spring of 1893 and who died some months later. In what amounts to an artistic manifesto, Proust dismissed the fragments in his book as the empty froth on a life which had been agitated but which was now settled down (aged twenty-four!). He promises to wait until the day when the surface of life's water is so calm and limpid that the muses themselves can admire their reflections, and see their own smiles and dances. This promise, broadly speaking, was kept.

– A.N. Wilson, 2004

The best commentary on Proust's first published work, *Pleasures and Days,* can be found in his mature masterpiece *In Search of Lost Time;* more precisely at the end of *The Guermantes Way.* The last ten or so pages of this volume (like many of Proust's cadences) is a set piece of great formal sophistication and thematic richness. A prolonged moment of social comedy is interwoven with the darker theme of illness and death. The narrator has come to see M. and Mme de Guermantes, partly in order to find out whether he really has been invited to a reception at the home of the Princesse de Guermantes; and while he waits in a staircase for them to return home from Cannes, he contemplates the lovely roofscape of Paris – the chimneys, all pink and red, make him think of tulips, and the windows across the courtyard frame their occupants like Dutch paintings. While waiting, he also makes an observation of crucial importance for his understanding of life, the revelation of which to the reader he leaves until later. When the Duc de Guermantes arrives, he is (as so often) bluffly jovial but at the same time edgy, partly because he knows that his cousin is dying – and if news of his death arrives, the Duc will be forced to relinquish the various pleasures that await him later the same day, including a fancy-dress ball where he will appear as Louis XI, and a rendezvous with his mistress. His wife the Duchesse is getting dressed to go out, and while he waits, he converses with the narrator: their discussion reveals the prejudices and obsessions of the aristocratic caste that has all the 'titles' but none of the real power enjoyed by its ancestors. Charles Swann arrives; an elegant member of the upper bourgeoisie, and something of a mentor to the narrator, he has managed by his intelligence, charm, sensitivity and artistic connoisseurship to gain access to the ranks of the aristocracy in spite of the fact that he is Jewish (we are in the middle of the Dreyfus Affair and the text refers several times to the way this has split French society). The narrator is shocked to see how ill Swann looks. Eventually, the Duchesse appears, in an elegant red dress for the evening's outing; Swann and the narrator share their admiration for her beauty. After some further chit-chat about artistic matters, as the Duc is starting to show his impatience to head off to dinner, the Duchesse tells

Swann of a planned spring holiday in Italy and Sicily: how wonderful it would be if he could accompany them as an artistic guide! Swann demurs, the Duchesse insists; eventually, with the greatest reluctance, Swann tells the Duchesse that the reason he can't go with them is that he will by then be dead – the doctors have told him he has only a few months to live, and may indeed die at any minute. The Duchesse gazes at him with her melancholy blue eyes. Just as the Duc shrugs off the imminent demise of his cousin, lest it interrupt his pleasures, so the Duchesse, with slightly more compunction, simply doesn't know how to cope with the stark alternative of showing pity for the dying Swann or being late for dinner. She hesitates. The Duc gets irritated and claims that their hostess, Mme de Sainte-Euverte, hates people to be late: the Duchesse, continuing to dither, starts to climb into the waiting carriage, whereupon the Duc notices that she is still wearing her black shoes, which clash with that gorgeous red dress. Completely ignoring what he has just said about the need for punctuality, he insists that she go upstairs and fetch her red shoes – what does it matter if they are late! And then, sensing that his fussing over the shoes might seem rather ill-judged, he hurries Swann and the narrator away, again resorting to bland denial of the inconvenient facts of impending mortality as he cheerfully tells Swann not to listen to the doctors, who are donkeys. 'You're as strong as the Pont-Neuf! You'll bury the lot of us!'

All the preoccupations of this passage can be traced back to *Pleasures and Days.* The narrator's musings over the roofs of Paris, his love of floral metaphor, his interest in reading art (especially Dutch art) into life (hence the 'picturesque' qualities of his description), the tendency to a kind of prose poetry, are already evident in the *Pleasures*, especially in the sequence called 'Nostalgia'. The discovery he makes while waiting in the staircase involves – as we will read at the beginning of the next volume, *Sodom and Gomorrah* – the revelation of the whole underworld of homosexuality that is to play an increasingly important part in the *Search*; and while the theme of sexual inversion is only briefly alluded to in *Pleasures and Days* (the apparently lesbian advance in 'Violante', for instance), sexuality itself – insistent, hot-housed, nervy, obsessive – is everywhere; in 'The Confession of a Young Woman', the heroine's wayward desires lead to her mother's death and her own protracted suicide (the *mise-en-scène* is quite clumsy and melodramatic, but Proust is already struggling to express an idea onto which the *Search* would train its spotlights: that the peculiar guilt attendant on sexuality is linked, in his view, with the profanation of the mother). Throughout *Pleasures and Days* there is no love that is not pathological, not least because of the paranoid intensity of the characters' jealousy. It is not so much that people are jealous because they are in love: they are in love because they are jealous (they only realise that they are in love, really and truly and catastrophically, when jealousy's little green claws start to dig into their hearts) – love is an epiphenomenon of a deeper possessiveness: this is the painful lesson learnt by Baldassare Silvande, and Françoise de Breyves, and Honoré in 'The End of Jealousy'. The passage I have quoted from *The Guermantes Way* is not specifically concerned with this most Proustian of emotions, but it *does* hold up to unremitting examination what might be called social jealousy – otherwise known as snobbery. The Duc de Guermantes is obsessed by matters of aristocratic precedence that can have only the most trivial impact in the 'real' world of modernity, but there is hardly a character in Proust who is not touched by this vice, and *Pleasures and Days* is already mercilessly analysing the hold of snobbery over the lives of its characters, most notably in the vignettes (often inspired by those observers of life at the Court of Louis XIV, La Bruyère and La Rochefoucauld) of 'Fragments from Italian Comedy'. It is true that the *Pleasures* often focus on these themes (lyrical evocation, sexuality, jealousy, snobbery) one at a time, whereas the *Search* shows how interrelated they are. But already some of the earlier texts display the dynamic interplay between and within them, just as they demonstrate a dialectical appreciation of the way that characters often have the strengths of their weaknesses, and learn what virtues they may have through vice. Thus while jealousy in some ways binds us to a life of suffering, the lessons it teaches may begin to offer us secret (and painfully acquired) strategies of detachment. Conversely, while many of the epigrams to the *Pleasures*, from *The Imitation of Christ* and other edifying texts, admonish us to seek precisely this detachment, to flee world, flesh and devil, the texts themselves suggest again that it may be attachment taken to its paroxysm that can best start to emancipate us from those very same temptations. There can be no songs of authentic innocence without experience. None of the characters in the *Pleasures* succeed in heeding the voice of conscience, the summons to an authentic solitude – all long country walks and fireside meditations; each of them succumb to 'mondanité', the worldliness of social existence. But through this worldliness (the gossip, the malice, the jaded cynicism) they learn things that no amount of Emersonian self-reliance would have taught them. Proust's early text proclaims a detachment and autonomy that have to be learnt the hard way, by living life to the full, undergoing experiences in the world that might seem to be pleasurable but have their own strange ascesis (from the deserts of love to the ordinary rituals of everyday social life: at the end of the extract from the *Search* I mentioned above, the Duchesse reflects that sometimes she'd rather just *die* than have to go out to dinner – and one can see why). Again, snobbery is dreadful, but what is worse is to try and pretend that you are *not* a snob (a denial that, again, almost all of Proust's characters make at one time or another – it is a guilty secret on a par with homosexuality). Furthermore, as the 'Fragments from Italian Comedy' show, people labour to achieve their snobbish ends with the same resourcefulness as an artist, and they learn as much about the world through their often comic endeavours as the jealous person does through being brought face to face with the radical unknowability of the loved one. The world comes alive (in a perverse way, no doubt, but still very intensely) when you are a snob: like the artist and the jealous lover, the snob lives for details – for a pair of red shoes, in the case of the Duchesse.

And not only the Duchesse. The young Proust begins and ends his *Pleasures* with stories that, although uncertain in tone, still manage to be searing depictions of the loneliness of death ('Baldassare Silvande' has been compared with Tolstoy's 'The Death of Ivan Ilych', though it does not have – does anything? – the pity and awe of the great Russian story); the mature Proust, amid the social ballet of the end of *The Guermantes Way,* shows how ineptly his characters cope with (or simply ignore) impending mortality. How crassly selfish are the Duc and Duchesse de Guermantes in the way they brush off Swann's announcement of his imminent death! And yet, here again, the text is more dialectical than it seems, and the *Search* is more consistently nuanced in its 'lessons' (lessons that, despite a tendency to theorising, to the essayistic, work best when seen as inseparable from the moment and mode of their discovery and the needs and limitations of their discoverer) than *Pleasures and Days*, which have an occasional tendency to the didactic, to the unsituated aphorism or maxim, or the wagging of a moralistic finger (but then, Proust was still only a very young man). When someone you love (and the affection of the Guermantes for Swann is, in spite of everything, quite real) announces that he will soon be dead, it is not only the Duchesse who can't find the right words to say in the little book of etiquette she carries around in her head. What *do* you say to the dying? How would delaying her own pleasures actually help Swann? And while all the bother over her outfit may seem to turn her into a Wicked Witch ('I *must* have those red slippers!'), a monster of egotism, it is not only her husband who has noticed she's still wearing her black shoes: Swann may be dying, but in all his dying he has spotted it too (and is still refined enough in his aesthetic appreciation not to be shocked by her somewhat daring, if involuntary, fashion statement). Even on the edge of the void, he *notices* things (in 'The End of Jealousy', Honoré on his deathbed will notice the buzzing fly and wonder idly whether it will land on the bed-sheet): it is not that the aesthetic (or the mere being-there of things) is trivialised by the proximity of death, that majestic abstract universal; it gains in intensity and perhaps value from it. They are indeed cruel in their thoughtlessness, these foolish and self-obsessed characters; but Swann has chosen to live by the code of worldliness and he dies by it too – being as he is 'polite' enough to realise that individual people come and go, but dinners in town go on for ever. The Duchesse's uncertain blue eyes seem to express a will to 'live all you can' that communicates with something in Swann himself, and whose power he acknowledges, like the epiphany of some demanding and yet strangely intimate deity. And one day, like Swann, they will all die, even the Duc and the Duchesse de Guermantes, and perhaps their attention for detail will be tenderly remembered: 'ah, the fuss he made when his wife went out improperly dressed! What an eye for detail he had! Husbands have their uses, you know!'

True, Proust does not spare the denizens of his world from moral condemnation: *saeva indignatio* is never far away. In one of the texts in the *Pleasures* ('A Dinner in Town'), he details the fatuous preoccupations of a group of well-heeled diners and their casual and ignorant tattle about the recent anarchist attacks, and he comments that not one of them had an income of less than a hundred thousand pounds. Brecht once commented that Kafka, for all his mysticism, was the truest Bolshevik of them all: it would be a little simplistic to summon Proust to the barricades too, but the link between class and sensibility is precisely documented in the *Search*, and his embrace of the aristocracy could be perfectly murderous: he was the archetypal 'smiler with the knife under the cloak' (or with a pen under the voluminous folds of his many layers of overcoats, as he tottered out from his cork-lined room to carry out fieldwork for his novel in the Ritz). The complex syntax, those long sentences with their coiling clauses that he was already practising in the *Pleasures* (with varied success – many of these pieces were dashed down in a couple of spare hours and never revised) is deployed in the *Search* to make us slow down and take the time to notice the world and the richness of its interconnections. But this slowness is not just that of wistful elegy (the doe-eyed Marcel gazing out of all those photographs with such infinite nostalgia). It conceals a message of extreme urgency, like the prophets at their most lapidary: 'all compound things are subject to decay', 'seek out your end with diligence', 'repent!' Like the Rilke poem which presents us with an 'Archaic Torso of Apollo', it concludes 'you must change your life'. Not for nothing did Proust consider calling his vast epic *La Colombe poignardée*, for his meditative sentences often launch a dove into the air (in his Preface to the *Pleasures* he makes much of the need to venture forth from the maternal Ark) only to stab it to death. The aesthetic has its decorative moment, but it is in the service of a stringent and at times alarming ethic – one in which truth seems achievable only through purgatorial detachment from life. Flaubert, the Flaubert of 'l'art pour l'art', is supposed to have returned from a routine social visit in an unusually reflective mood: 'ils sont dans le vrai', he said of the family he had just seen. (He was not usually so mellow about ordinary life.) But Proust sometimes thought art itself was a way of living in the truth.

Sometimes this produces a certain triumphalism. When in the *Search* the writer Bergotte dies after visiting an exhibition of Vermeer paintings, the narrator imagines that his books, opened in the windows of the bookshops as a tribute to him, are like a sign of his resurrection. The appropriation of religious imagery in such a context, and the use of sacramental language in Proust's work as a whole (the 'petite madeleine' that in *Swann's Way* signals the living return of the apparently dead past – like its namesake Mary Magdalen), may give us pause: the Bergotte episode is made more poignant and personal by the fact that it is the near transcription of Proust's own experience, since he himself attended a Vermeer exhibition shortly before his death – there is, as it were, a delightfully modest little cough and a questioning, smiling 'me too?' in this meditation on the immortality of the artist, and it is all kept in a relatively low key (the rococo rustle of those angels with their paper wings…). The negative side of this is the way that, from the *Pleasures* to the very end of the *Search*, Proust seems at times to be adumbrating the idea that *only* artists (the 'creative') are saved: it's the cork-lined room and the three-thousand page epic or nothing – thus says the Gospel of Saint Marcel. There is harshness as well as empathy in his attitude towards the failures and wasters he depicts, starting with Baldassare Silvande and Violante and Honoré in the *Pleasures* and extending to almost everyone in the *Search*. Art is a strenuous deity, much less forgiving than other gods; and the service of art, he seems to be saying, is the only authentic life in a world given over to illusion and gossip and what Pascal called 'divertissement'. But it is far from sure that this is really a creed that can be deduced from Proust's work as a whole (he could be just as harsh on the 'idolaters' of art as on the philistines; and while philistinism is a shame, idolatry is a sin). The epigrams of the *Pleasures*, and the theorising of the *Search,* are one thing, but the text itself indicates something quite different. Proust's characters, whether or not they are artists, whether or not they find some truth amid the trivia, whether they are callous and footling time-servers or examples of the most solicitudinous loving-kindness (the Narrator's mother and grandmother in the *Search*), have what dignity they have, not because of the way they look at life but because of the way they are looked at by others (as the *Pleasures* repeatedly point out, we are often quite unaware of the effect we have on other people, who may understand our lives better than we do) – looked at by one other in particular, by the novelist who notices everything, and for whom, as for Kierkegaard, all things are fraught with mystery, from the Incarnation to the buzzing of a fly – or the importance of wearing the 'right' shoes. His characters live because he has brought them into being: his eye (the eye of someone simply more human than most of us) has rested on them and seen them for what they are. The clarity of this gaze, which through its tenderness, amusement and indignation cares even about those who have signally failed to live in the truth, has something maternal about it.

– Andrew Brown, 2004

Note on the Text:
I used the text of *Les Plaisirs et les jours* contained in the volume *Jean Santeuil*, ed. by Pierre Clarac and Yves Sandre (Paris: Gallimard, 'Pléiade', 1971). I was able to consult with great profit the fine translation by Louise Varese (*Pleasures and Regrets*: Peter Owen, London, 1986; tr. first published 1948).

This translation is dedicated, with much love, to the memory of my mother (d. January 2004).

Pleasures and Days

Why did he ask me to present his book to curious minds? And why did I promise to take on this highly agreeable but quite unnecessary task? His book is like a young face full of rare charm and elegant grace. It is self-recommending, tells us about itself and presents itself in spite of itself.

True, it is a young book. It is young as its author is young. But it is an old book too, as old as the world. It is the spring of leaves on ancient branches, in the age-old forest. One is tempted to say that the new shoots are saddened by the long past of the woods and are wearing mourning for so many dead springs.

The grave Hesiod recited his *Works and Days* to the goatherds of Helicon. It is a more melancholy task to recite *Pleasures and Days* to our high society gentlemen and ladies, if, as the well-known English man of state claims, life would be quite tolerable if it were not for pleasures. So our young friend's book has weary smiles and postures of fatigue that are deprived neither or beauty nor of nobility.

Even his sadness will be found to be pleasing and full of variety, conducted as it is and sustained by a marvellous spirit of observation, and a supple, penetrating and truly subtle intelligence. This calendar of *Pleasures and Days* marks both the hours of nature, in its harmonious depictions of the sky, the sea and the woods, and the hours of humankind in its faithful portraits and its genre paintings, with their wonderful finish.

Marcel Proust delights equally in describing the desolate splendour of the sunset and the agitated vanities of a snobbish soul. He excels in recounting the elegant sorrows and the artificial sufferings that are at least the equal in cruelty of those which nature showers on us with maternal prodigality. I must confess that I find these invented sufferings, these pains discovered by human genius, these sorrows of art, enormously interesting and valuable, and I am grateful to Marcel Proust for having studied and described a few choice examples.

He lures us into a greenhouse atmosphere and detains us there, amid wild orchids that do not draw the nourishment for their strange and unhealthy beauty from this earth. Suddenly there passes, through the heavy and languid air, a bright and shining arrow, a flash of lightning which, like the ray of the German doctor, can go right through bodies. At a stroke the poet has penetrated secret thoughts and hidden desires.

This is his manner, and his art. He here shows a sureness of touch surprising in such a young archer. He is not at all innocent. But he is so sincere and so authentic that he appears naive, and as such we like him. There is something in him of a depraved Bernardin de Saint-Pierre and an ingenuous Petronius.

What a fortunate book is his! It will go all round the town adorned and perfumed by the flowers strewn on it by Madeleine Lemaire, with that divine hand which scatters the roses with their dew.

– Anatole France
Paris, 21st April 1896

TO MY FRIEND WILLIE HEATH

Died in Paris 3rd October 1893

> *From the lap of God in which you rest…*
> *reveal to me those truths which conquer*
> *death, prevent us from fearing it and*
> *almost make us love it.*

The ancient Greeks brought cakes, milk and wine for their dead. Seduced by a more refined illusion, if not by one that is any wiser, we offer them flowers and books. If I am giving you this one, it is first and foremost because it is a book of images. Despite the 'legends', it will be, if not read, at least looked at by all the admirers of that great artist who has given me, without any affectation, this magnificent present, the woman of whom we might well say, adapting Dumas's words, 'that she is the one who has created the most roses after God'. M. Robert de Montesquiou has also celebrated her, in poems as yet unpublished, with that ingenious gravity, that sententious and subtle eloquence, that rigorous form which at times in his work recalls the seventeenth century. He tells her, speaking of flowers:

> *Posing for your paintbrush encourages them to bloom […]*
> *You are their Vigée[1] and you are Flora too,*
> *Who brings them immortality, where she brings only doom!*

Her admirers are an elite, and there is a host of them. It was my wish that on the first page they should see the name of the man they had no time to become acquainted with and whom they would have admired. I myself, dear friend, knew you for only a very short time. It was in the Bois de Boulogne that I would often meet you in the mornings: you had spotted me coming and were waiting for me beneath the trees, erect but relaxed, like one of those great lords painted by Van Dyck, whose pensive elegance you shared. And indeed their elegance, like yours, resides less in clothes than in the body, and their bodies seem to have received it and to continue ceaselessly to receive it from their souls:

5

it is a moral elegance. And everything, moreover, helped to bring out that melancholy resemblance, even the background of foliage in whose shadow Van Dyck often caught and fixed a king taking a stroll; like so many of those who were his models, you were soon to die and in your eyes as in their eyes one could see alternately the shades of presentiment and the gentle light of resignation. But if the grace of your pride belonged by right to the art of a Van Dyck, you were much closer to Leonardo da Vinci by the mysterious intensity of your spiritual life. Often, your finger raised, your eyes impenetrable and smiling at the sight of the enigma you kept to yourself, you struck me as Leonardo's John the Baptist. Then we came up with the dream, almost the plan, of living more and more with each other, in a circle of magnanimous and well-chosen men and women, far enough from stupidity, vice and malice to feel safe from their vulgar arrows.

Your life, as you wished it to be, would comprise one of those works of art which require a lofty inspiration. Like faith and genius, we can receive this inspiration from the hands of love. But it was death that would give it to you. In it too and even in its approach reside hidden strength, secret aid, a 'grace' which is not found in life. Just like lovers when they start to love, like poets at the time when they sing, those who are ill feel closer to their souls. Life is hard when it wraps us in too tight an embrace, and perpetually hurts our souls. When we sense its bonds relaxing for a moment, we can experience gentle moments of lucidity and foresight. When I was still a child, no other character in sacred history seemed to me to have such a wretched fate as Noah, because of the flood which kept him trapped in the ark for forty days. Later on, I was often ill, and for days on end I too was forced to stay in the 'ark'. Then I realised that Noah was never able to see the world so clearly as from the ark, despite its being closed and the fact that it was night on earth. When my convalescence began, my mother, who had not left me, and would even, at night-time, remain by my side, 'opened the window of the ark', and went out. But, like the dove, 'she came back in the evening'. Then I was altogether cured, and like the dove 'she returned not again'. I had to start to live once more, to turn away from myself, to listen to words harder than those my mother spoke; what was more, even her words, perpetually gentle until then, were no longer the same, but were imbued with the severity of life and of the duties she was obliged to teach me. Gentle dove of the flood, seeing you depart, how can one imagine that the patriarch did not feel a certain sadness mingling with his joy at the rebirth of the world? How gentle is that suspended animation, that veritable 'Truce of God' which brings to a halt our labours and evil desires! What 'grace' there is in illness, which brings us closer to the realities beyond death – and its graces too, the graces of its 'vain adornments and oppressive veils', the hair that an importunate hand 'has carefully gathered', the soft mild acts of a mother's or friend's faithfulness that so often appeared to us wearing the very face of our sadness, or as the protective gesture that our weakness had implored, and which will stop on the threshold of convalescence; often I have suffered at feeling that you were so far away from me, all of you, the exiled descendants of the dove from the ark. And who indeed has not experienced those moments, my dear Willie, in which he would like to be where you are? We assume so many responsibilities towards life that there comes a time when, discouraged at the impossibility of ever being able to fulfil them all, we turn towards the tombs, we call on death, 'death who comes to the aid of destinies that are difficult to accomplish'. But if she unbinds us from the responsibilities we have assumed towards life, she cannot unbind us from those we have assumed towards ourselves, the first and foremost in particular – that of living so as to be worth something, and to gain merit.

More serious than any of us, you were also more childlike than anyone, not only in purity of heart, but in your innocent and delightful gaiety. Charles de Grancey had a gift which I envied him, that of being able, with memories of your schooldays, to arouse all of a sudden that laughter that never slumbered for long within you, and that we will hear no more.

If some of these pages were written at the age of twenty-three, many others ('Violante', almost all the 'Fragments from Italian comedy', etc.) date from my twentieth year. All of them are merely the vain foam of a life that was agitated but is now calming down. May that life one day be limpid enough for the Muses to deign to gaze at themselves in it and for the reflection of their smiles and their dances to dart across its surface!

I am giving you this book. You are, alas! the only one of my friends whose criticism it had nothing to fear from. I am at least confident that nowhere would its freedom of tone have shocked you. I have depicted immorality only in persons of a delicate conscience. Thus, as they are too weak to will the good, too noble to indulge with real enjoyment in evil, knowing nothing but suffering, I have managed to speak of them only with a pity too sincere for it not to purify these short essays. May that true friend, and that illustrious and beloved Master who have added the poetry of his music and the music of his incomparable poetry respectively, and may M. Darlu too, that great philosopher whose inspired spoken words, more assured of lasting life than anything written, have in me as in so many others engendered thought, forgive me for having reserved for you this last token of my affection, bearing in mind that no one living, however great he may be or however dear, must be honoured before one who is dead.

THE DEATH OF BALDASSARE SILVANDE
VISCOUNT OF SYLVANIA

1

The poets say that Apollo tended the flocks
of Admetus; so too, each man is a God in
disguise who plays the fool.
(Emerson)

'Monsieur Alexis, don't cry like that, maybe the Viscount of Sylvania
will give you a horse.'

'A big horse, Beppo, or a pony?'

'A big horse, perhaps, like Monsieur Cardenio's. But please don't cry
like that... on your thirteenth birthday!'

The hope that he might be getting a horse, and the reminder that he
was thirteen years old today, made Alexis's eyes shine through their
tears. But he was not entirely consoled, since it would mean having
to go and see his uncle, Baldassare Silvande, Viscount of Sylvania.
Admittedly, since the day he had heard that his uncle's illness was
incurable, Alexis had seen him several times. But since then, everything
had completely changed. Baldassare had realised how ill he was and
now knew that he had at most three years to live. Alexis could not
understand how this certainty had not already killed his uncle with
grief, or driven him mad, and for his own part felt quite unable to bear
the pain of seeing him. Convinced as he was that his uncle would start
talking to him about his imminent demise, he did not think he had the
strength to hold back his own sobs, let alone console him. He had
always adored his uncle, the tallest, most handsome, youngest, liveliest,
most gentle of all his relatives. He loved his grey eyes, his blond
moustache, and his knees – a deep and welcoming place of pleasure
and refuge when he had been smaller, seemingly as inaccessible as a
citadel, affording him as much enjoyment as any wooden horse, and
more inviolable than a temple. Alexis, who openly disapproved of
his father's sombre and severe way of dressing, and dreamt of a future in
which, always on horseback, he would be as elegant as a fine lady and

as splendid as a king, recognised in Baldassare the most ideal man imaginable; he knew that his uncle was handsome, and that he himself resembled him, and he knew too that his uncle was intelligent and noble-hearted, and wielded as much power as a bishop or a general. It was true that his parents' criticisms had taught him that the Viscount had his failings. He could even remember the violence of his anger on the day when his cousin Jean Galeas had made fun of him, how much the gleam in his eyes had betrayed the extreme pleasure of his vanity when the Duke of Parma had offered his sister's hand in marriage to him (on that occasion he had clenched his jaws in an attempt to disguise his pleasure and pulled a face, an expression habitual to him – one that Alexis disliked), and he remembered too the tone of contempt with which his uncle spoke to Lucretia, who professed not to like his music.

Often, his parents would allude to other things his uncle had done, things which Alexis did not know about, but which he heard being severely censured.

But all of Baldassare's failings, including the vulgar face he pulled, had certainly disappeared. When his uncle had learnt that in two years, perhaps, he would be dead, how much the mockeries of Jean Galeas, the friendship of the Duke of Parma and his own music must have become a matter of indifference to him!... Alexis imagined him to be just as handsome, but solemn and even more perfect than he had been before. Yes, solemn, and already no longer altogether of this world. Thus his despair was mingled with a certain disquiet and alarm.

The horses had long been harnessed, and it was time to go; he climbed into the carriage, then stepped back out, as he wanted to go over and ask his tutor for one last piece of advice. At the moment he spoke, he turned very red.

'Monsieur Legrand, is it better if my uncle thinks or does not think that I know that he is going to die?'

'Better that he does not think so, Alexis!'

'But what if he starts talking about it?'

'He won't talk about it.'

'He won't talk about it?' said Alexis in surprise, for this was the only possibility he had not foreseen: each time he had started imagining his visit to his uncle, he had heard him speaking of death to him with the gentleness of a priest.

'Yes but, what if he *does* talk about it?'

'You'll tell him he's wrong.'

'And what if I start crying?'

'You've cried enough this morning, you won't cry when you're at his place.'

'I won't cry!' exclaimed Alexis in despair, 'but he'll think I'm not sorry about it, that I don't love him… my dear old uncle!'

And he burst into tears. His mother, tired of waiting, came to fetch him; they set off.

When Alexis had given his little overcoat to a valet in white and green livery, with the Sylvanian coat of arms, who was standing in the entrance hall, he paused for a moment with his mother to listen to a violin melody coming from a nearby room. Then they were led into a huge round room, with windows extending all around it, where the Viscount was often to be found. As you went in, you saw the sea facing you and, as you looked round, lawns, pastures, and woods were visible; at the far end of the room, there were two cats, roses, poppies, and a great number of musical instruments. They waited for a while.

Alexis suddenly rushed over to his mother. She thought he wanted to kiss her, but he asked her in a low voice, his mouth glued to her ear, 'How old is my uncle?'

'He'll be thirty-six in June.'

He wanted to ask, 'Do you think he'll ever actually make thirty-six?' but he did not dare.

A door opened, Alexis trembled, and a servant said, 'The Viscount will be here presently.'

Soon the servant returned, ushering in two peacocks and a kid goat that the Viscount took everywhere with him. Then they heard some more footsteps and the door opened again.

'It's nothing,' Alexis told himself; his heart thumped every time he heard a noise. 'It's probably a servant, yes, most probably a servant.' But at the same time he heard a gentle voice saying, 'Hello, young Alexis, many happy returns of the day!'

And his uncle came to kiss him, and made him feel afraid – and no doubt realised as much, since he turned away to give him time to pull himself together, and started to chat cheerfully to Alexis's mother, his sister-in-law, who, ever since the death of his mother, had been the person he loved most in the world.

Alexis, now feeling reassured, felt only immense affection for this young man, still so charming, scarcely any paler, and so heroic as to be able to adopt a tone of cheerfulness during these tragic minutes. He would like to have flung his arms around him but did not dare, fearing that he might break his uncle's composure and cause him to lose his self-possession. It was the Viscount's sad and gentle eyes that especially made him want to cry. Alexis knew that his eyes had *always* been sad and that, even at the happiest times, he seemed to be imploring you to console him for sorrows that apparently did not affect him. But just now, he felt that his uncle's sadness, bravely banished from his conversation, had taken refuge in his eyes, the only sincere thing about his whole appearance, together with his hollowed cheeks.

'I know you'd like to drive a two-horse carriage, young Alexis,' said Baldassare. 'Tomorrow they'll bring you a horse. Next year, I'll make up the complete pair and in two years, I'll give you the carriage. But perhaps this year you'll already be able to ride the horse, we'll try it out when I get back. I'm leaving tomorrow, you see,' he added, 'but not for long. I'll be back within a month and we can go off together and, you know, see a matinee of that comedy I promised to take you to.'

Alexis knew that his uncle was going to spend a few weeks at one of his friends' houses. He also knew that his uncle was still allowed to go to the theatre; but as he was even now transfixed by the idea of death that had so deeply shaken him before coming to his uncle's, the latter's words gave him a painful and profound surprise.

'I won't go,' he said to himself. 'How much pain it would cause him to hear the actors' buffoonery and the audience's laughter!'

'What was that lovely violin tune we heard when we came in?' asked Alexis's mother.

'Ah! so you thought it was lovely?' said Baldassare quickly, looking extremely pleased. 'It was the romance I mentioned to you.'

'Is he putting it on?' Alexis wondered. 'How can the success of his music still give him any pleasure?'

Just then, the Viscount's face assumed an expression of deep pain; his cheeks had grown pale, he pursed his lips and knit his brows, and his eyes filled with tears.

'Good Lord!' thought Alexis in alarm, 'he's not up to playing this part! Poor uncle! Anyway, why is he so concerned to spare us any suffering? Why take such a burden on himself?'

But the painful effects of his general paralysis, which sometimes gripped Baldassare as if in an iron corset, even imprinting marks and bruises on his body, and whose intensity had just forced him to contort his face despite his best efforts, had vanished.

He resumed his good-humoured conversation, after wiping his eyes.

'I have the impression the Duke of Parma has been rather neglecting you of late?' Alexis's mother asked, unthinkingly.

'The Duke of Parma?' exclaimed Baldassare in tones of rage, 'the Duke of Parma, neglecting me? But what can you be thinking of, my dear? This very morning he wrote to me to put his castle in Illyria at my disposal, if I think the mountain air will do me any good.'

He suddenly stood up, but this brought on another attack of his dreadful pain, and he had to keep still for a while; his suffering had hardly been assuaged before he summoned a servant.

'Bring me the letter next to my bed.'

And he made haste to read:

My dear Baldassare,
How sorry I am not to be able to see you, etc.

As the Prince came out with more and more kindly words, Baldassare's face softened, and shone with happiness and confidence. Suddenly, no doubt because he wished to disguise a joy that he felt was not very dignified, he clamped his teeth together and made the attractive and rather vulgar little grimace that Alexis had imagined forever banished from his face, pacified as it was by death.

This little grimace, now twisting Baldassare's lips as it had before, opened the eyes of Alexis who, ever since he had been in his uncle's presence, had thought and hoped that he would be able to contemplate the face of a dying man forever detached from vulgar realities – a face

13

on which the only expression would be the gentle hint of a heroically forced smile, tender and melancholy, heavenly and disenchanted. Now his doubts had been removed, and he knew that Jean Galeas, by teasing his uncle, had yet again made him angry, and that in the sick man's gaiety, in his desire to go to the theatre, there was no trace of either pretence or courage, and that now that he was on the threshold of death, Baldassare still continued to think only of life.

On his return home, Alexis was overwhelmed by the thought that he too would one day die, and that even if he himself still had much more time ahead of him than his uncle, the latter's old gardener and his cousin, the Duchess of Alériouvres, would certainly not survive Baldassare for long. And yet, even though he was wealthy enough to retire, Rocco continued to work ceaselessly so as to earn even more money, and was trying to win a prize for his roses. The Duchess, in spite being seventy years old, took great care to dye her hair and paid for newspaper articles in which the youthfulness of her bearing, the elegance of her receptions, and the refinements of her table and her wit were all celebrated.

These examples did nothing to diminish the sudden amazement that his uncle's attitude had aroused in Alexis, but rather gave him a kindred feeling that, gradually spreading, turned into an immense stupefaction at the universal scandal of these existences, his own included, walking backwards into death with their gaze still fixed on life.

Resolved not to imitate such a shocking aberration, he decided, following the ancient prophets of whose renown he had been taught, to retire to the desert with some of his close friends, and he communicated this wish to his parents.

Happily, more powerful than their derision, life itself, whose sweet and fortifying milk he had not yet drunk dry, proffered her breast to dissuade him. And he settled back to drink from it anew, with an avid joy whose insistent grievances his credulous and fertile imagination took with naive seriousness, and whose dashed hopes that same imagination made amends for so magnificently.

2

The flesh is sad, alas…
(Stéphane Mallarmé)

The day after Alexis's visit, the Viscount of Sylvania had left for the nearby château for a stay of three or four weeks: the presence of numerous guests might take his mind off the melancholy that often followed his attacks of ill health.

Soon all the pleasures he enjoyed there came to be concentrated in the company of a young woman who made them twice as intense by sharing them with him. He thought he could sense that she was in love with him, but kept her at a certain distance: he knew she was absolutely pure, and was in any case impatiently awaiting her husband's arrival; and then, he was not sure he really loved her, and felt vaguely what a sin it would be to lead her into temptation. When exactly their relationship had become less innocent he was never able to recall. Now, as if by virtue of a tacit understanding, which had come into existence at some indeterminate period, he would kiss her wrists and stroke her neck. She seemed so happy, that one evening he went further: he started by kissing her; then he caressed her at length and once more kissed her on her eyes, her cheek, her lips, her neck and the wings of her nose. The young woman's lips puckered up with a smile to meet his caresses, and her eyes shone in their depths like a pool of water warmed by the sun. Meanwhile, Baldassare's caresses had become bolder; one minute he gazed at her; he was struck by her pallor, by the infinite despair expressed by her lifeless brow, her weary, grief-stricken eyes shedding glances sadder than tears, like the torture endured during crucifixion or after the irremediable loss of someone you love. He gazed at her for a while; and then, in one final effort, she raised up to him her suppliant eyes begging for mercy, while her avid lips, in an unconscious, convulsive movement, asked for yet more kisses.

Both of them were rapt in the pleasure that hovered all around them, in the perfume of their kisses and the memory of their caresses, and they flung themselves on one another, but with their eyes now closed, those cruel eyes that showed them their souls' distress, a distress they refused to see – he in particular kept his eyes shut tight, with all his strength, like a remorseful executioner sensing that his arm might waver when the times comes to strike his victim, aware of the risk he would run if, instead of imagining her as still arousing and thus forcing him to assuage the wrath she aroused, he were to look into her face and for a moment feel her pain.

Night had fallen and she was still in his room, dry-eyed, her gaze wandering. She left without saying a word, kissing his hand with passionate melancholy.

He however could not sleep, and if he did momentarily doze off, he would come to with a start, sensing his sweet victim's eyes raised towards him, imploring and desperate. All at once, he imagined her as she now must be, also unable to sleep and feeling so very lonely. He got dressed, walked quietly to her room, not daring to make any noise in case he woke her, should she be asleep, not daring, either, to go back to his room, where heaven and earth and his own soul would suffocate him under their weight. He stood there, just outside the young woman's room, each moment thinking that he would be unable to contain himself a second longer and would have to walk in; then, horrified at the idea of breaking that sweet oblivion in which she slept – breathing softly, sweetly and evenly, as he could hear – only to deliver her cruelly over to the remorse and despair from whose grip she had, for a moment, found repose, he remained there, at her door, sometimes sitting, sometimes kneeling, sometimes lying down. In the morning, he returned to his room, feeling the chill, and calmer now; he slept for a long time and woke up in a state of great well-being.

They found ingenious ways of mutually allaying each other's conscience, and grew used to the remorse which faded and to the pleasure which also lost its edge, and when he returned to Sylvania, he retained, as did she, no more than a gentle, somewhat frigid memory of those cruel and fiery moments.

3

When Alexis, on his fourteenth birthday, went to see his uncle Baldassare, he did not feel, as he had expected he would, the violent emotions of the previous year. His repeated rides on the horse his uncle had given him had imbued him with new strength, and overcome his tendency to nervous exhaustion, reviving in him that uninterrupted feeling of good health which supplements our youth like the obscure awareness of the depths of our resources and the latent powers of our vitality. As he felt his chest swelling like a sail in the breeze awoken by his gallop, his body burning like a winter fire and his forehead as cool as the fleeting foliage that wreathed it in passing, and as he stretched out his body under a cold shower, or allowed it to relax at length as he savoured the meal he was digesting, he would exalt in those inner powers of life which, having once been the tumultuous pride of Baldassare, had forever withdrawn from him and come to bring new joy to younger souls, whom they would also, nonetheless, one day desert.

Nothing in Alexis could now suffer with his uncle's debility or die at his imminent demise. The joyous buzz of the blood in his veins and the desires in his head prevented him from hearing the sick man's ever fainter plaints. Alexis had entered on that ardent period when the body labours so energetically to build palaces between itself and the soul that the latter soon seems to have disappeared – until the day when illness or grief have slowly opened a painful fissure, through which the soul again appears. He had grown used to his uncle's fatal illness, as we become used to everything around us that lasts for a certain time; and even though his uncle was still alive, since he had once made Alexis weep for the same reason that the dead always make us weep, he had behaved towards Baldassare as if he had actually been dead, and had begun to forget him.

When, on that particular day, his uncle had said to him, 'Young Alexis, I'm giving you the carriage at the same time as the second horse,' he had realised that his uncle was thinking, 'as otherwise you'd risk never having the carriage at all', and he knew that this was an extremely sad thought. But he did not feel it to be such, as just now he had no more room within himself for any deep sadness.

A few days later, while reading, he was struck by the depiction of a villain who had been left unmoved by the most touching and tender affection of a dying man who adored him.

That evening, he was kept awake by the fear of being the villain in whom he had thought he could recognise himself. But the following day, he had such a lovely ride out on his horse, worked so well, and in addition felt so much affection for his living parents that he fell back into the habit of enjoying life without scruple, and sleeping without remorse.

Meanwhile, the Count of Sylvania, who was starting to lose his ability to walk, barely left his château any more. His friends and relatives spent all day with him, and he could confess to the most blameworthy folly or the most absurd extravagance, parade the most shocking paradox or hint at the most shocking failing, without his relatives uttering a word of reproach, or his friends allowing themselves to make a joke or contradict him. It seemed that he had been tacitly relieved of the responsibility for his deeds and words. It seemed in particular that, by swathing his ailments in their kindness, and even vanquishing them with their caresses, they were trying to stop him from hearing the last creaks and groans of his body as life departed from it.

He would spend long, delectable hours lying down and holding intimate conversations with himself, the only guest he had neglected to invite to supper during his lifetime. As he pampered his long-suffering body, and leaned in resignation at the window gazing out to sea, he felt a melancholy joy. He decorated the scene of his death with images of this world – images which surged up within him but which distance, already detaching him from them, turned into something hazy and beautiful; and this deathbed scene, long premeditated but endlessly embellished and renewed with ardent melancholy, was like a work of art. Already he had sketched out in his mind's eye his farewells to the Duchess Oliviane, his great Platonic friend, over whose salon he reigned, even though the greatest lords, the most renowned artists and the most brilliant people in Europe had gathered there. He felt as if he could already read the account of their last conversation:

'…The sun had set, and the sea, visible between the apple trees, was mauve. As light as weightless, withered wreaths, and as persistent as regrets, little blue and pink clouds were floating on the horizon. A melancholy row of poplar trees was immersed in shadow, their resigned heads bathed in a pink glow like that of a church; the last rays of the sun, without touching their trunks, dyed their branches and, from those balustrades of shadow, draped garlands of light. The breeze mingled the three aromas of sea, damp leaves and milk. Never had the Sylvanian countryside tempered the melancholy of evening with a more alluring tenderness.

' "I loved you so much, but I gave you so little, my poor dear," she told him.

' "What do you mean, Oliviane? You gave me so little, you say? You gave me all the more in that I asked you for less – much more, to be honest, than if sensual pleasure had played any part in our affections. Supernatural as a madonna, gentle as a nurse – I loved you and you rocked me in your arms. I loved you with a tenderness whose delicate forbearance no expectation of carnal pleasure ever came to ruffle. Did you not bring me, in exchange, incomparable friendship, exquisite tea, conversation both natural and ornate, and how many bouquets of fresh roses? You alone were able, with your maternal, expressive hands, to cool my burning, fevered brow, to pour honey into my withered lips, and fill my life with noble images.

' "My dear friend, give me your hands so I may kiss them…" '

Only the indifference of Pia, a little Princess from Syracuse, whom he still loved with all his senses and with his whole heart and who had fallen for Castruccio with a wild and invincible love, occasionally brought him back him to a crueller reality, albeit one which he strove to forget. Right up to the final days, he had still been present at parties where, as he walked along arm in arm with her, he thought he was humiliating his rival; but even then, at her side, he sensed that her deep eyes were distracted by another love that only her pity for a sick man made her try to disguise. And now he could not even manage this. He had so lost control of the movement of his legs that he was now unable to go out. But she would often come to see him, and as if she had entered the great conspiracy of kindness woven by the others, she would talk to him constantly with an ingenious affection that was no longer shown to be feigned, as it once had been, by her exclamations of indifference or the open expression of her anger. And he felt this gentle attentiveness, more than all the others, filling his whole being with its solace and delight.

But one day, as he was rising from his chair to go to table, his servant was amazed to see him walking with much more self-assurance. He summoned the doctor, who said he needed to wait before giving his verdict. The next day he was walking well. After a week, he was allowed to go out. His friends and relatives were then filled with an immense hope. The doctor thought that a simple and curable nervous disease had perhaps been the initial cause of the symptoms of general paralysis – which was now, indeed, starting to disappear. He presented his doubts to Baldassare as a certainty, and told him, 'You are saved!'

The man who had been sentenced to death expressed deep joy and emotion on learning that he had been pardoned. But after a while, as his recovery continued to make progress, a persistent note of disquiet started to make itself heard beneath the joy that had already started to fade as he grew used to it. Sheltered from life's storms, in that propitious atmosphere of all-pervasive gentleness, enforced calm and untrammelled meditation, deep within him the seed of an obscure desire for death had started to grow. He was still far from suspecting its existence, and merely felt a vague panic at the thought of having to start living again, having to suffer the blows which he had lost the habit of enduring, and being forced to lose the caresses that had recently enfolded him. He was also dimly aware that it would be wrong to lose himself in pleasure or action, now that he had learnt to know himself, and become acquainted with the fraternal stranger who, as he watched the boats furrowing the sea, had conversed with him for hours on end, far away, so close, within him. As if now he were sensing an as yet unknown love, newly born, awakening within him, like a young man who has been deceived about his true original homeland, he felt a longing for death, for which he had once felt he was setting out as if into eternal exile.

He ventured an idea, and Jean Galeas, who knew he was cured, contradicted him violently and teased him. His sister-in-law, who for two months had been visiting him every evening and morning, went for two days without coming to see him. It was too much! For too long he had lost the habit of bearing life's burdens, and he no longer wished to pick them up again. And this was because life had not managed to recapture him with her charms. His strength returned, and with it all his desire to live; he went out, started living once more, and died to himself a second time. After a month, the symptoms of general paralysis reappeared. Little by little, just as before, walking became difficult and then impossible for him, but gradually enough for him to grow accustomed to his return to death, so that he now had time to avert his gaze from it. His relapse did not even have the advantage of the first attack – *then*, he had eventually begun to detach himself from life, no longer seeing it in its reality, but gazing on it, like a picture. Now, conversely, he was becoming vainer, more irritable, pierced by longing for the pleasures he could no longer enjoy.

His sister-in-law, whom he loved tenderly, was the only one who brought some solace to his final days, coming to see him several times a day, with Alexis.

One afternoon, as she was going to see the Viscount, just as she was drawing up to his house, the horses of her carriage suddenly took fright; she was violently flung out, trampled by a horseman who was galloping by, and brought into Baldassare's house unconscious, with her skull split open.

The coach driver, who had not been wounded, immediately came to announce the accident to the Viscount, whose face turned waxen with shock and anger. His teeth were clenched, his eyes flashed and bulged and, in a terrible outburst of wrath, he hurled prolonged abuse at the coach driver; but it seemed as if these explosions of violence were an attempt to disguise a cry of pain which, in the intervals, could faintly be heard. It was as if, next to the infuriated Viscount, there was a sick man lamenting. Soon this plaint, at first feeble, stifled his cries of anger, and he fell onto a chair, sobbing.

Then he wanted to have his face washed so that his sister-in-law would not be alarmed by the traces of his grief. His servant shook his head sadly; the wounded woman had not regained consciousness. The Viscount spent two desperate days and nights at his sister-in-law's side. At any moment she might die. On the second night, a hazardous operation was attempted. On the morning of the third day, her fever had fallen, and the patient smiled as she looked at Baldassare who, unable to hold back his tears any longer, wept uninterruptedly for joy. While death had been approaching him little by little, he had refused to see it; now he had found himself suddenly in its presence. It had terrified him by threatening what he held most dear; he had begged it for mercy, and he had forced death to yield.

He felt strong and free, proudly sensing that his own life was not as precious to him as was that of his sister-in-law, and that he could view it with so much scorn now that she, a different person, had filled him with pity. It was death, now, that he could look in the face, and not the scenes he had imagined would accompany that death. He wanted to remain as he now was right up to the end, and no longer give in to the lie which, by trying to arrange a fine and splendid deathbed agony for him, would have thereby committed the last and worst of its profanations, sullying the mysteries of his death just as it had hidden from him the mysteries of his life.

4

Tomorrow, and tomorrow, and tomorrow,
Creeps in this petty pace from day to day,
To the last syllable of recorded time –
And all our yesterdays have lighted fools
The way to dusty death. Out, out, brief candle!
Life's but a walking shadow; a poor player
That struts and frets his hour upon the stage,
And then is heard no more: it is a tale
Told by an idiot, full of sound and fury,
Signifying nothing.
(Shakespeare, *Macbeth*)

The stress and upheaval Baldassare had experienced during his sister-in-law's illness had accelerated his own malady. He had just heard from his confessor that he had less than a month to live; it was ten o'clock in the morning, and it was pouring with rain. A carriage stopped outside the château. It was Duchess Oliviane. When he had been making those artistic arrangements for the scene of his death, he had told himself:

'…it will happen on a clear evening. The sun will have set, and the sea, visible between the apple trees, will be mauve. As light as weightless, withered wreathes, and as persistent as regrets, little blue and pink clouds will be floating on the horizon…'

It was ten in the morning, under a lowering, filthy sky, as the rain came pelting down, when Duchess Oliviane arrived; and, worn out by his illness, his mind entirely given over to higher things, and no longer susceptible to the grace of all that had once seemed to constitute the value, the charm, the splendour and refinement of life, he asked them to tell the Duchess that he was not strong enough to see her. She insisted, but he refused to receive her. And this was not even out of a sense of duty: she meant nothing to him any more. Death had made short work of breaking those bonds whose capacity to enslave him he had for some weeks so greatly feared. When he tried to think of her, he saw nothing appear before his mind's eye, and the eyes of his imagination and his vanity had closed.

However, about one week before his death, the announcement of a ball to be given by the Duchess of Bohemia, at which Pia was to lead the cotillion with Castruccio who was leaving for Denmark the next day, reawoke his jealousy in all its fury. He asked for Pia to come to him; his sister-in-law resisted his request for a while; he thought that they were preventing him from seeing her, that they were persecuting him; he flew into a rage, and so as not to torment him further, they immediately sent for her.

When she arrived, he was completely calm, but in a deep state of sadness. He drew her over to his bed and immediately started talking to her about the Duchess of Bohemia's ball. He told her:

'We were not related, you won't need to go into mourning for me, but I wish to beg one thing of you: promise me you won't go to that ball.'

They gazed into one another's eyes from which their souls seemed to peer out – those melancholy, passionate souls that death had not succeeded in uniting.

He understood her hesitation, pressed his lips together painfully and gently told her:

'Oh! it's better if you don't promise! Don't break a promise made to a dying man. If you're not sure you can keep your promise, don't make one.'

'I can't promise you that, I haven't seen him for two months and I may never see him again; nothing would ever console me, in all eternity, if I didn't go to that ball.'

'You're right, since you love him, and death may happen any minute… and you are still living life to the full… But you will do one little thing for me; during the time you spend at the ball, set aside the period that you'd have been obliged to spend with me so as to divert suspicion from you. Invite my soul to remember for a few moments, together with you – spare some thought for me.'

'I hardly dare promise you that, the ball will last such a short time. Even if I don't leave his side, I will hardly have time to see him. I'll set aside some time for you on all the days that follow.'

'You won't be able to, you'll forget me; but if, after one year – alas! more than that, perhaps – something sad that you read, someone's death, or a rainy evening make you think of me, what charity you will be doing me! I'll never, ever see you again… except in spirit, and for that to happen, we'd need to be thinking of each other simultaneously. *I* will think of you always, so that my soul will always be open to you, if you wish to enter it. But how long the guest will keep me waiting! The November rains will have rotted the flowers on my tomb, June will have withered them, and my soul will still be weeping with impatience. Ah! I hope that one day, the sight of some souvenir, the return of an anniversary, the drift of your thoughts will lead your memory into the neighbourhood of my tenderness; then it will be as if I had heard you and spotted you coming, and some magic spell will have decked everything out with flowers for your arrival. Think of the dead man. But, ah! – can I hope that death, and your own sense of the gravity of things, will accomplish what life, with all its passion, and all our tears, and our moments of gaiety, and our lips could not?'

5

Now cracks a noble heart; good night,
sweet prince;
And flights of angels sing thee to thy rest!
(Shakespeare, *Hamlet*)

Meanwhile, a violent fever accompanied by delirium refused to loosen its grip on the Viscount; a bed had been made up for him in the vast rotunda where Alexis had seen him on his thirteenth birthday, when he had still been so cheerful, and from which the sick man could now look out over the sea and the harbour jetty and at the same time, on the other side, the pastures and the woods. Now and then, he would start to speak; but his words no longer bore the trace of those thoughts of higher things that, over the last weeks, had purified him with their visit. In violent imprecations against some invisible person who kept teasing him, he insisted over and over again that he was the finest musician of his century and the greatest lord in the universe. Then, suddenly calming down, he would tell his coach driver to take him to some humble lodge and have his horses saddled up for hunting. He asked for writing paper to invite to dinner all the sovereigns of Europe on the occasion of his marriage with the sister of the Duke of Parma; alarmed that he might not be able to pay off a gambling debt, he would seize the paperknife placed near his bed and level it in front of him like a revolver. He would send out messengers to find out whether the policeman he had beaten up the previous night was dead, and he would utter obscenities to a person whose hand he thought he was holding. Those exterminating angels called Will and Thought were no longer there to thrust back into the shadows the evil spirits of his senses and the foul emanations of his memory. After three days, at around five o'clock, he awoke as you wake from some bad dream for which you are not responsible, but which you indistinctly remember. He asked if any friends or relatives had been near him during those hours in which he had presented only the most negligible, most primitive and most lifeless side of himself, and he begged his servants, if he were again overcome by delirium, to show those acquaintances out and allow them back in only when he had regained consciousness.

He lifted his eyes, looked around the room, and gazed with a smile at his black cat which, having climbed onto a china vase, was playing with a chrysanthemum and sniffing the flower with the gestures of a mime artist. He asked everyone to leave and talked for a long time with the priest who was watching over him. Nonetheless, he refused to take communion and asked the doctor to explain that his stomach was no longer in any fit state to tolerate the Host. After an hour, he asked his servant to tell his sister-in-law and Jean Galeas to go home. He said:

'I am resigned; I am happy to die and to go before God.'

The air was so mild that they opened the windows that looked over the sea, yet without seeing it; and because of the rather fresh breeze they left the ones opposite closed, those facing the expanse of pasture and woodland.

Baldassare had his bed pulled over to the open windows. A boat was being launched from the jetty, where sailors were hauling it along by rope. A handsome cabin boy, about fifteen years old, was leaning forward, right at the edge; at every wave he looked as if he were going to fall into the water, but he stood firm on his sturdy legs. He was holding out the net with which he would catch the fish, and a lighted pipe was clamped between his lips that could taste the salty tang of the sea. And the same wind that swelled the sail came to cool the cheeks of Baldassare, and made a piece of paper flutter round the room. He turned away his head from the happy image of the pleasures that he had passionately loved and would never enjoy again. He looked at the harbour: a three-master was setting sail.

'It's the ship leaving for India,' said Jean Galeas.

Baldassare could not make out the people standing on the deck, waving their handkerchiefs, but he could guess at the thirst for the unknown that filled their eyes with longing; *they* still had so much to experience, to know, and to feel. The anchor was weighed, a cry went up, and the boat moved out over the sombre sea to the West, where, in a golden haze, the light mingled the small boats together with the clouds and murmured irresistible and vague promises to the travellers.

Baldassare had the windows on this side of the rotonda closed, and those looking out over the pastures and the woods opened. He gazed at the fields, but he could still hear the cry of farewell from the three-master, and he could see the cabin boy, with his pipe between his teeth, holding out his nets.

Baldassare's hand fidgeted feverishly around. Suddenly he heard a faint silvery sound, imperceptible and profound like a beating heart. It was the sound of the bells from a village in the far distance, which, thanks to the gracious and kindly air, so limpid this evening, and the favourable breeze, had crossed many leagues of plains and rivers before reaching him and being detected by his faithful ears. It was a voice both present and very ancient; now he could hear his heart beating with the bells' melodious flight, hanging on the moment when they seemed to breathe the sound in, and then breathing out a long slow breath with them. At every period in his life, whenever he had heard the distant sound of the bells, he had involuntarily remembered the gentle sound they made in the evening air when, still a small child, he would make his way back to the château, across the fields.

At that moment, the doctor asked everyone to draw near, saying:

'It's the end!'

Baldassare was resting, his eyes closed, and his heart listening to the sound of the bells that his ears, paralysed by the approach of death, could no longer hear. He saw his mother again – the way she would give him a kiss when she got home, and then put him to bed at night and warm his feet in her hands, staying at his side if he couldn't get to sleep; he remembered his *Robinson Crusoe* and the evenings in the garden when his sister would sing; the words of his tutor predicting that one day he would be a great musician, and his mother's delight at the time, which she tried in vain to hide. Now he had run out of time to realise the passionate hopes of his mother and his sister, hopes that he had so cruelly dashed. He saw the lime tree under which he had become engaged and the day when his engagement had been broken off, when only his mother had been able to console him. He imagined he was hugging his old maidservant and holding his first violin. He saw all of this in the distance, glowing sweetly and sadly like the horizon which the windows facing the fields looked towards and yet did not see.

He saw all of this, and yet two seconds had not elapsed since the doctor, listening to his heart, had said:

'It's the end!'

He straightened, saying:

'It's all over!'

Alexis, his mother and Jean Galeas knelt down, together with the Duke of Parma who had just arrived. The servants wept outside the open door.

– October 1894

VIOLANTE, OR HIGH SOCIETY

1

The meditative childhood of Violante

> *Have little commerce with young people
> and those in society... Do not yearn to
> appear in the company of the great.
> (The Imitation of Christ, I, 7)*

The Viscountess of Syria was noble-hearted and tender, and she charmed all around her with her grace. Her husband the Viscount had a very lively wit, and the features of his face were admirable in their regularity. But the least grenadier was more sensitive and less vulgar than he was. Far from the world, in the rustic domain of Styria, they brought up their daughter Violante, who, as attractive and lively as her father, and as charitable and mysteriously alluring as her mother, seemed to combine her parents' qualities into a perfectly proportioned and harmonious whole. But the changing aspirations of her head and her heart did not encounter any force of will within her which might, without limiting them, have guided them and prevented her from becoming their charming and fragile plaything. This lack of willpower caused Violante's mother anxieties which might, in time, have borne fruit, if the Viscountess had not, together with her husband, perished violently in a hunting accident, leaving Violante orphaned at the age of fifteen. Living almost alone, under the vigilant but quite unskilled guardianship of old Augustin, her tutor and the bailiff of the château of Styria, Violante, for lack of friends, found in her dreams charming companions to whom she promised to remain faithful all her life long. She would take them for walks along the avenues in the grounds, and through the countryside, and bade them lean with her on the terrace which, bordering the domain of Styria, overlooks the sea. Brought up by them to rise, as it were, above herself, and initiated by them into life, Violante acquired a taste for the whole visible world, and a foretaste of the invisible. Her joy was boundless, interrupted by moments of sadness so sweet that they surpassed her joy in intensity.

2

Sensuality

> *Do not lean on a reed blown in the wind and do not place your trust in it, for all flesh is as grass and its glory passes like the flower of the fields.*
> (*The Imitation of Christ*)

Apart from Augustin and a few children from the district, Violante never saw anyone. Only a younger sister of her mother's, who lived at Julianges, a château a few hours' journey away, sometimes came to pay Violante a visit. One day when she was visiting her niece, one of her friends came with her. His name was Honoré and he was sixteen. Violante did not like him, but he came back. As they strolled along an avenue in the grounds, he told her some extremely improper things, which she had never yet guessed at. She experienced a very agreeable pleasure at the thought of them, but immediately felt ashamed. Then, as the sun had set and they had been walking for a long time, they sat down on a bench, doubtless so as to gaze at the reflections of the pink sky, soft and mild on the sea. Honoré moved close up to Violante so she would not get cold, fastened the fur round her neck with an ingenious slowness, and suggested that she try and put into practice, with his help, the theories that he had just been telling her about as they walked through the grounds. He tried to speak softly to her, and brought his lips up to Violante's ear; she did not move away; but they heard a rustle in the undergrowth.

'It's nothing,' said Honoré, tenderly.

'It's my aunt,' said Violante.

It was the wind. But Violante had already risen to her feet, and feeling – just in time – a salutary chill from this gust of wind, did not want to sit down again and took her leave of Honoré, despite his pleadings. She felt remorse for this later, had a fit of nerves, and for two days in succession took a very long time in getting to sleep. The memory of him was a burning pillow which she kept turning over and over again. Two days later, Honoré asked to see her. She sent him a message to say that she had gone out for a walk. Honoré did not believe her, and did not dare return. The following summer, her thoughts returned to Honoré with tenderness, but also with sadness, since she knew he had gone off to sea as a sailor. When the sun had sunk into the sea, as she sat there on the bench to which he had, a year ago, led her, she kept trying to remember Honoré's proffered lips, his half-closed green eyes, his gaze, roaming here and there like rays of sunshine, and resting on her with a little of their warm and living light. And during the mild nights, the vast and secretive nights, when the certainty that no one could see her aroused her desire, she heard Honoré's voice murmuring forbidden things into her ear. She imagined him in his entirety – an obsessive memory, proffered to her like a temptation. One evening, at dinner, she gazed at the bailiff sitting opposite her and sighed.

'I'm so sad, my dear Augustin,' said Violante. 'Nobody loves me,' she added.

'But,' replied Augustin, 'a week ago, when I went to Julianges to sort out the library, I heard someone talking about you and saying, "How lovely she is!" '

'Who said so?' said Violante, gloomily.

The ghost of a languid smile hardly raised one corner of her mouth, as when you try to lift a curtain to let in the cheerful daylight.

'That young man from last year, Monsieur Honoré…'

'I thought he'd gone to sea,' said Violante.

'He's back,' said Augustin.

Violante stood up immediately and, almost tottering on her feet, made her way up to her room to write to Honoré and tell him to come and see her. As she picked up her pen, she was filled with an unprecedented feeling of happiness and power, the feeling that she was arranging her life at her own whim and for her own pleasure; she felt that, in spite of the cogs of their two destinies which seemed to keep them mechanically imprisoned far from one another, she could all the same give that mechanism a little flick with her thumb: he would appear at night, on the terrace, quite different in appearance from the way the cruel ecstasy of her unslaked desire represented him; her unheeded affections – the novel perpetually being written inside her – and the force of circumstance really were linked by avenues of communication, and she could rush down them towards the impossible that she would convert into a possibility by creating it. The following day she received Honoré's reply, and took it the bench where he had embraced her, and where she now read it, trembling.

> *Mademoiselle,*
> *I have just received your letter, one hour before my ship's departure.*
> *We had put into port for just a week, and I will return only in four*
> *years' time. I humbly hope that you will keep in your memory*
> > *Your respectful and affectionate*
> > *Honoré*

Then, gazing out on that terrace to which he would never return, where no one would ever come to satisfy her desire, and on the sea also that had stolen him from her and in exchange suffused him, in the young girl's imagination, with some of its own great allure, mysterious and melancholy, the allure of things that do not belong to us, that reflect too many skies and wash around too many shores, Violante burst into tears.

'My poor Augustin,' she said that evening, 'a great misfortune has befallen me.'

The initial need to share confidences sprang in her case from the first obstacles placed in the path of her sensuality, just as naturally as it usually springs from the first satisfactions of love. She had still not known love. Shortly afterwards, she suffered its pains – which is the only way we ever get to know it.

The pains of love

Violante had fallen in love: in other words, a young Englishman by the name of Laurence was for several months the object of her most trivial thoughts, and the goal of her most important actions. She had gone out hunting with him and could not understand why the desire to see him again now enslaved her mind, impelled her to go out to meet him, and kept sleep far from her, destroying her happiness and peace of mind. Violante was in love: her love was scorned. Laurence loved the world: she loved him and longed to follow him. But Laurence would not spare a glance for this twenty-year-old country girl. She fell ill with resentment and jealousy, and went off to take the waters at … to try and forget him; but her self-esteem was wounded at seeing him prefer to her so many other women who were not her equal – and she was resolved on acquiring all their advantages for herself so that she could triumph over them.

'I'm leaving you, my dear Augustin,' she said, 'and going to the Austrian Court.'

'Heaven forbid!' said Augustin. 'The poor folks around here will no longer be consoled by your charity once you're surrounded by so many wicked people. You won't play with our children in the woods. Who will be our church organist? We won't see you out painting in the countryside, and you won't be here to compose songs for us.'

'Don't worry, Augustin,' said Violante, 'just make sure my château and my Styrian peasants remain handsome and faithful to me. Society is just a means to an end. It gives you commonplace but invincible weapons, and if I hope to be loved one day, I need to possess them. I am also impelled by a certain curiosity, almost a need, to lead a somewhat more material and less reflective life than the one I lead here. It's both a rest and an education I'm after. As soon as my position is assured and my holiday over, I will leave society for the countryside, and come back to our good simple folk and what I prefer above all else, my songs. At a precise moment, not too far in the future, I will stop going down that particular path and return to this Styria of ours to live with you, my dear.'

'Will you be able to?' said Augustin.

'One can do whatever one wants,' said Violante.

'But maybe you won't want the same things,' said Augustin.

'Why?' asked Violante.

'Because you will have changed,' said Augustin.

4

High Society

Society people are so dull that Violante merely had to condescend to mingle with them to eclipse almost all of them. The most remote and lofty lords, and the most unruly artists, all came of their own accord to pay her court. She alone had wit, taste, and a demeanour which awoke the idea of every perfection. She inspired plays, perfumes and dresses. Dressmakers, writers and hairdressers came begging for her protection. The most famous modiste in Austria asked her permission to be called her personal hat-maker, and the most illustrious prince in Europe asked her permission to be called her lover. She felt it was her duty to refuse both of them this mark of esteem which would have definitively put the seal on their elegance. Among the young people who asked to be received in Violante's home, Laurence drew attention to himself by his persistence. Having caused her so much sorrow, he now inspired in her a certain repugnance. And his fawning made her keep her distance even more than all the scorn for her that he had shown.

'I have no right to get angry,' she said to herself. 'I hadn't loved him out of consideration for his greatness of soul, and I sensed perfectly clearly, without admitting it to myself, that he was a base fellow. That didn't stop me loving him, but it did stop me loving greatness of soul as much as I should have done. I thought it was possible to be both base and loveable at the same time. But once you've fallen out of love, you go back to preferring people with a bit of feeling. How strange it was, my passion for that wretch – it was entirely cerebral, and didn't have the excuse of being led astray by the senses! Platonic love doesn't amount to much.' We shall see that she would shortly come to the conclusion

34

that sensual love amounted to even less.

Augustin came to see her, and tried to persuade her to go back to Styria with him.

'You have conquered a veritable kingdom,' he told her. 'Isn't that enough for you? Why don't you turn back into the old Violante?'

'Yes, I have indeed just conquered a kingdom, Augustin,' replied Violante. 'At least let me enjoy my conquest for a few months.'

An event that Augustin had not foreseen meant that Violante could dispense for a while with any thought of retirement. After having rejected twenty most serene highnesses, the same number of sovereign princes and a man of genius who had asked for her hand, she married the Duke of Bohemia who had the most dazzling charm and five million ducats. The announcement of Honoré's return almost caused the marriage to be broken off the day before it was due to be celebrated. But an illness to which he had succumbed had disfigured him and made his familiarities appear hateful to Violante. She wept over the vanity of her desires which had once winged their ardent way to the flesh that had then been in its first bloom and was now withered forever. The Duchess of Bohemia continued to charm everyone just as Violante of Styria had done, and the Duke's huge fortune merely served to set the work of art that she now was within a frame worthy of her. Having been a work of art she became a luxury item, by virtue of that tendency, natural to things here below, which makes them sink down to the lowest level unless some noble effort maintains, so to speak, their centre of gravity above themselves. Augustin was astonished at all the things he heard about her.

'Why,' he wrote to her, 'does the Duchess spend her time talking about the same things that Violante so despised?'

'Because I would be less popular if I expressed preoccupations which, by their very superiority, are neither liked nor understood by people in high society,' replied Violante. 'But I'm bored, my dear Augustin.'

He came to see her, and explained to her why she was bored.

'Your liking for music, for reflection, for charity, for solitude, for the countryside, can no longer find any outlet. You are obsessed by success and held in thrall by pleasure. But one can find happiness only by doing what one loves in the depths of one's soul.'

'How do you know that? You've never lived,' said Violante.

'I've thought. That's life enough,' said Augustin. 'But I hope you will soon be seized by disgust at this insipid way of life.'

Violante felt more and more bored, and was now incapable of showing enjoyment. Then the immorality of society, which until now had left her indifferent, assailed her and wounded her cruelly, just as the harshness of the seasons overwhelms bodies deprived by illness of their capacity to fight back. One day that she was out walking by herself along an almost deserted avenue, from a carriage she had not at first noticed there stepped out a woman who came straight up to her. This woman stopped her, and asked her whether she was indeed Violante of Bohemia, whereupon she told her that she had been her mother's friend and had felt a desire to see once more the little Violante she had once held on her knees. She kissed her with deep feeling, put her arm round her waist and started kissing her so repeatedly that Violante, without even saying goodbye, took to her heels in flight. On the evening of the next day, Violante went to a party given in honour of the Princess of Misenum, whom she did not know. On seeing the Princess, she recognised her as the abominable woman of the previous day. And a dowager, whom Violante had hitherto thought highly of, said to her:

'Would you like me to introduce you to the Princess of Misenum?'

'No!' said Violante.

'Don't be shy,' said the dowager. 'I'm sure she'll take a liking to you. She's very fond of pretty women.'

From that day onward, Violante had two deadly enemies, the Princess of Misenum and the dowager, who both depicted her to everyone as a monster of pride and perversity. Violante discovered this, and wept for herself and the wickedness of women. She had long since resigned herself to the wickedness of men. Soon she was telling her husband every evening:

'We're setting out the day after tomorrow for my beloved Styria, and we will never leave it again.'

Then along came a party that, maybe, she would enjoy more than the others, and a prettier dress to show off. The deep need to imagine, to create, to live by herself in thought alone, and thus to dedicate herself to something, while it made her suffer at the fact that it was still unfulfilled, and while it prevented her from finding in society even a shadow of joy, had become too dulled, and was no longer imperious enough to make her change her way of life, or to force her to renounce the world and realise her true destiny. She continued to present the sumptuous and desolate spectacle of an existence made for the infinite and little by little restricted to next to nothing, filled only with the melancholy shadows of the noble destiny she might have fulfilled, but which she neglected ever more each day. The deep surge of charity that might have washed her heart like a great wave, levelling all the human inequalities that clog a worldly heart, was held back by the thousand dikes of egotism, coquetry and ambition. Even kindness seemed to her laudable only as an elegant gesture. She would perform many more charitable deeds, lavishing money and even time and effort, but a whole part of herself was held captive, and no longer belonged to her. She would still read or dream as she lay in bed in the mornings, but her mind was warped, and now came to a halt on the exterior of things; when it paid itself any attention at all, it was not in order to understand itself more profoundly, but to admire itself, voluptuously and coquettishly, as if in a mirror. And if anyone had come to announce visitors, she would not have had the will power to send them away so that she could continue dreaming or reading. She had reached such a state that she could no longer enjoy nature other than with perverted senses, and the charm of the seasons now existed for her only as an extra perfume for her elegant social appearances, for which it set the tone. The charms of winter became the pleasure of feeling the cold, and the enjoyment of hunting closed her heart to the melancholy of autumn. Sometimes she would go walking by herself through a forest, trying to rediscover the natural source of all true joys. But, even under the shady leaves, she insisted on wearing eye-catching dresses. And the pleasure of her elegance ruined for her the joy of being alone and able to dream.

'Are we setting off tomorrow?' the Duke would ask.

'The day after tomorrow,' Violante would reply.

Eventually the Duke stopped asking. When Augustin lamented her absence, Violante wrote, 'I'll come back when I am a little older.'

'Ah!' replied Augustin, 'you are deliberately lavishing your youth on them; you will never return to your Styria.'

She never did return. In her youth, she had remained in society to reign over that kingdom of elegance which, while still almost a child, she had conquered. In her old age, she remained in society to defend that kingdom. In vain. She relinquished it. And when she died, she was still trying to reconquer it. Augustin had reckoned that weariness would wean her away. But he had not reckoned on a force which, if it is at first fed by vanity, vanquishes weariness, contempt, and even boredom: the force of habit.

– August 1892

> *...As crabs, goats, scorpions, the balance*
> *and the water pot lose their meanness*
> *when hung as signs in the zodiac, so I can*
> *see my own vices without heat in... distant*
> *persons.*
> (Emerson)

1

Fabrizio's mistresses

Fabrizio's mistress was intelligent and beautiful; nothing could console him for this fact. 'She shouldn't know her own mind so well!' he groaned aloud, 'I find her beauty is spoiled by her intelligence; would I still fall in love with the Mona Lisa each time I looked at her, if I had to listen at the same time to some critic sounding off, however exquisitely?' He abandoned her, and took another mistress who was beautiful and devoid of wit. But she continually prevented him from enjoying her charm, thanks to her merciless lack of tact. Then she aspired to intelligence, read a great deal, became pedantic and was just as intellectual as the first woman, but less naturally, and with a ridiculous clumsiness. He begged her to keep quiet: even when she was not talking, her beauty cruelly reflected her stupidity. Finally, he struck up an acquaintance with a woman whose intelligence could be guessed at merely through her more subtle grace: she was happy just to live, and did not dissipate in cavilling conversations the alluring mystery of her nature. She was as gentle as the gracious, agile beasts with their deep gaze, and troubled people's minds like the morning memory, poignant and vague, of their dreams. But she could not be bothered to do for him what the two others *had* done – namely, love him.

Countess Myrto's lady friends

Myrto, pretty, witty and kind, but with a weakness for everything that's in vogue, prefers Parthenis over her other lady friends; Parthenis is a Duchess and has a more brilliant social life than does Myrto; and yet she enjoys the company of Lalagé, whose elegance is the exact equal of hers, and she is not indifferent to the agreeable sides of Cleanthis, who is of humble rank and does not lay claim to any distinction. But a woman Myrto cannot stand is Doris; Doris's social position is just below that of Myrto, and she seeks out Myrto, as Myrto does Parthenis, for her greater elegance.

If we can observe these likes and dislikes on Myrto's part, the reason is that Duchess Parthenis not only procures certain advantages for Myrto, but can also love the latter for herself alone; Lalagé too can love her for herself, and in any case, as they are colleagues and on the same level, they need each other; and finally, by cherishing Cleanthis, Myrto feels with pride that she is capable of disinterested affection for someone, able to like them sincerely, understand them and love them – that, if necessary, she is elegant enough to do without elegance. Doris, on the other hand, merely expresses her desire for all that is in vogue, without being in a position to satisfy it; she comes to Myrto's like a little dog lurking near a big dog in the hope of snatching a bone from it; she wants to sniff out her duchesses and see if she can steal one of them for herself; she causes displeasure, as does Myrto, by the disagreeable disproportion between her real rank and the rank to which she aspires; she presents Myrto, in other words, with the mirror image of her vice. Myrto's friendship for Parthenis is the same as that which Myrto recognises with displeasure in the attentions that Doris pays to *her*. Lalagé, and even Cleanthis, reminded her of her dreams of ambition, and Parthenis at least was starting to realise them: Doris speaks to her only of her own pettiness. And so, too irritated to play the amusing role of protectress, she harbours for Doris exactly the same feelings which she, Myrto, would inspire in Parthenis, if Parthenis were not above snobbery: in other words, she hates her.

Heldemone, Adelgise, Ercole

Having witnessed a rather indelicate scene, Ercole does not dare to relate it to the Duchess Adelgise, but does not feel the same scruples in front of the courtesan Heldemone.

'Ercole,' exclaims Adelgise, 'do you really think that such a story isn't fit for my ears? Ah, I am sure that you would not behave the same way with the courtesan Heldemone. You respect me; you don't love me.'

'Ercole,' exclaims Heldemone, 'don't you have more of a sense of decency than to tell me that story? Just tell me – would you treat the Duchess Adelgise the same way? You don't respect me: so you can't possibly love me.'

4

Inconstancy

Fabrizio, who wants to love – and thinks he will love – Beatrice for ever, reflects that he wanted – and thought – the same when he loved, for six months at a time, Hippolyta, Barbara or Clelia. So he tries to find in the real qualities of Beatrice a reason to think that, once his passion ends, he will continue to frequent her home, since the thought that one day he might live without seeing her is incompatible with his feelings for her, feelings that have the illusion they will last for all eternity. Then, as a prudent egotist, he would not want to devote himself like this – concentrating on her his every thought, all his actions and intentions, and his plans for all possible futures – to the woman who shares only a few of his hours. Beatrice is keen-witted and a good judge. 'Once I have stopped loving her, what pleasure I will have in talking to her about others, about herself, and my dead love for her…' (which will thus revive, converted into a more durable friendship – he hopes). But, once his passion for Beatrice is over, he goes for two years without visiting her, without feeling any desire to do so, and without suffering at the thought that he feels no desire to do so. One day, when he is forced to go and see her, he curses, and stays there for just ten minutes. The reason is that he now dreams day and night of Giulia, who is singularly lacking in wit but whose pale hair smells as nice as some aromatic herb, and whose eyes are as innocent as two flowers.

5

Life is strangely easy and gentle for certain persons of great natural distinction, witty and affectionate, but capable of every vice, even though they exercise none of these vices in public, and even though it is impossible to say for sure that they are guilty of a single one of them. There is something supple and secretive about them. And then, their perversity adds a certain piquancy to the most innocent occupations, such as going for a walk in the garden at night.

6

Cires perdues

I

I saw you just now for the first time, Cydalise, and I immediately admired your blonde hair, which placed as it were a little golden helmet onto your childlike, pure and melancholy head. A dress of a somewhat pale red velvet softened that singular face even more, whose lowered eyes seemed to have sealed up forever some mystery within. But you lifted up your gaze; it rested on me, Cydalise, and into the eyes that I then saw there seemed to have flowed the fresh purity of mornings, the running waters of the first days of spring. They were like eyes which had never gazed on anything which human eyes are accustomed to reflect – eyes still virgin of earthly experience. But when I gazed at you more intently, you seemed above all to be expressing something full of love and suffering, like a woman to whom, even before birth, the fairies had refused what she would like to have possessed. The fabrics that you wore assumed on you a grace full of sorrow, adding a certain melancholy to your arms in especial, your arms that were just disconsolate enough to remain simple and charming. Then I imagined you as a princess come from far, far away, across the centuries, enduring the tedium of never-ending life here with a resigned languor – a princess dressed in clothes of rare and ancient harmony, the contemplation of which would soon have become a sweet and intoxicating habit for the eyes. I would like to have made you tell me of your dreams and your troubles. I would like to have seen you holding in your hand a goblet, or rather one of those flagons, so proud and melancholy in shape, which, now standing empty in our museums, and presenting in their useless grace the spectacle of a cup drained dry, were in bygone days, like you, a delightful refreshment on the tables of Venice, whose last violets and last roses have left a still floating memory in the limpid currents of their foaming, cloudy glass.

II

'How can you prefer Hippolyta to the five others I have just mentioned,' who are the most unquestionable beauties of Verona? To begin with, her nose is too long and too aquiline.' – You might add that her skin is too delicate, and her upper lip too thin: it pulls her mouth up excessively when she laughs, making too sharp an angle. And yet her laughter makes a huge impression on me, and the purest profiles leave me cold in comparison with the line of her nose, in your opinion too aquiline, but in my view so touching – it reminds me of a bird. Her head is also rather like a bird's, so long from her forehead to the blonde nape of her neck, and even more birdlike are her piercing and gentle eyes. Often, at the theatre, she will lean on the edge of her box; her arm in its white glove rises erect up to her chin, propped on her bent fingers. Her perfectly formed body fills out her habitual gauze dresses like folded wings. She makes you think of a bird standing dreaming on one elegant and slender leg. It is charming, too, to see her feather fan fluttering next to her, beating its white wing. I have never been able to see her sons or her nephews, who, like her, all have aquiline noses, thin lips, piercing eyes, and over-delicate skin, without being struck by the traces of her lineage, which doubtless issued from a goddess and a bird. Through the metamorphosis which today keeps some winged desire enchained in this feminine form, I can recognise the peacock's petite and regal head, though behind it there no longer billows the sea-blue, sea-green wave, or the foam of its mythological plumage. She gives one the idea of the fabulous, together with a frisson of beauty.

7

Snobs

I

A woman does not hide the fact that she likes balls, races, and even gambling. She says it straight out, or admits it quite simply, or even boasts about it. But don't try to get her to say that she likes whatever is in vogue: she would deny it indignantly, and get really angry. This is the only weakness that she takes care to hide, doubtless because it is the only one that humiliates one's vanity. She is happy to be dependent on the whim of cards, but not on that of dukes. Just because she commits some extravagance, she doesn't think that she is inferior to anyone; her snobbishness, on the other hand, implies that there *are* people to whom she is inferior, or might well become so, if she dropped her guard. And so we see a certain woman proclaiming that the question of what is or isn't in vogue is a completely stupid business, while lavishing on it the finesse, wit and intelligence that she could have employed on writing a fine short story or inventing some ingenious refinements in the pleasures and pains she gives her lover.

II

Women of wit are so afraid that someone might accuse them of liking what is in vogue that they never name it; if pressed in conversation, they resort to circumlocution to avoid having to name this potentially compromising lover. If need be, they jump at the name Elegance, which diverts suspicion and which at least seems to suggest that they organise their lives in accordance with artistic criteria rather than those of vanity. Only those women who are not yet in vogue or else are no longer so can name that quality, with all the ardour of unsatisfied or abandoned lovers. Thus it is that certain women launching themselves out onto the world or certain old women in their decline are happy to speak of the way others are in vogue, or, even better, *not* in vogue. Actually, if talking about the others not in vogue gives them the greater pleasure, talking about the others who really are so is meat and drink for them, providing their famished imaginations with, so to speak, more real and solid food. I have known some women for whom the thought of the brilliant relations a duchess had gained by marriage gave a frisson of pleasure even more than it aroused their envy. There are, it appears, out in the provinces, women shopkeepers whose skulls contain, as if locked up in a narrow cage, desires for whatever is in vogue that are as fierce and avid as wild beasts. The postman brings them *Le Gaulois*. Its news of the fashionable world is devoured in an instant. Those anxious provincial women are sated. And for a whole hour, their eyes, now bright and clear again, will shine all the more lustrously, filled to brimming with intense pleasure and admiration.

III

Against a snobbish woman

If you were not a member of high society, and someone told you that Élianthe – young, beautiful, rich, surrounded by the love of friends and lovers as she is – suddenly breaks off with them, indefatigably implores the favours of men, sometimes ugly, old and stupid, whom she hardly knows, and meekly suffers their rebuffs, labours as hard to please them as if she were undergoing penal servitude, is first crazy and then more sensible about them, makes herself their friend by her unbounded attentiveness to their needs, so that if they are poor she becomes their support, and if they are sensual, their mistress, you would think: what crime must Élianthe have committed, and who are these fearsome

45

magistrates that she must at all costs bribe, to whom she sacrifices her friendships, her love affairs, her freedom of thought, the dignity of her life, her fortune, her time, and her most intimate womanly aversions? And yet, Élianthe has committed no crime. The judges she insists on trying to bribe hardly even spared her a thought, and would have left her to spend her pure and cheerful life in calmness and tranquillity. But a terrible curse weighs upon her: she is a snob.

IV

To a snobbish woman

Your soul is indeed, in Tolstoy's turn of phrase, a deep dark forest. But the trees in it are of a particular species – they are genealogical trees. People say you're a vain woman? But for you the universe is not empty, but full of armorial bearings. This conception of the world is really rather brilliant and quite symbolic. Do not you, too, have your chimeras, shaped and coloured like those we see painted on coats of arms? Are you not well educated? *Tout-Paris*, *Gotha* and *High Life* have taught you your *Bouillet*.[2] While reading the story of the battles won by certain ancestors, you have come across the name of their descendants, whom you invite to dinner, and thanks to this mnemonics you have learnt by heart the entire history of France. Hence there is a certain grandeur in your ambitious dream, to which you have sacrificed your freedom, your hours of pleasure or meditation, your duties, your friendships, and love itself. For the faces of your new friends are accompanied in your imagination by a long series of portraits of their ancestors. The genealogical trees that you cultivate with such care, and whose fruits you pluck each year with so much joy, have roots which plunge deep into the most ancient French soil. Your dream establishes a sense of solidarity between present and past. For you, the soul of the crusades gives new life to quite ordinary contemporary faces, and if you reread your list of engagements so feverishly, is this not because, at every name, you sense awakening, tremulous and almost singing, like a dead woman arising from her emblazoned funereal slab, all the pomp and circumstance of old France?

Oranthe

You didn't go to bed last night and you still haven't had a wash this morning?

Why proclaim it aloud, Oranthe?

You are a man of brilliant gifts: don't you think they are enough to mark you out from everyone else? Do you feel that, in addition, you need to play such a melancholy role?

Your creditors are harassing you, your infidelities are driving your wife to despair, putting on evening dress would, for you, be tantamount to wearing livery, and nobody could ever force you to appear in society other than with your hair dishevelled. Sitting down to dinner, you do not take off your gloves to show that you are not eating, and at night, if you feel rather feverish, you have your victoria harnessed to go for a ride in the Bois de Boulogne.

You can read Lamartine only on nights when it has snowed, and listen to Wagner only if you can have cinnamon burnt at the same time.

And yet you are a decent chap, rich enough not to incur debts unless you thought they were necessary to your genius, affectionate enough to suffer when you cause your wife a pain that in your view it would be too bourgeois to spare her; you do not go out of your way to avoid company, you can make yourself popular with others, and your wit, even without your long curly hair, would attract quite enough attention. You have a healthy appetite, you eat well before you go out into town to dine, and yet it drives you mad to have to deprive yourself of food when you get there. At night, during the excursions which you undertake only out of a desire to seem original, you catch the only illnesses from which you ever suffer. You have enough imagination to make snow fall or to burn cinnamon without your needing winter or a perfume brazier, you are literate enough and musical enough to love Lamartine and Wagner in spirit and in truth. And yet! – to the soul of an artist you add all the bourgeois prejudices, showing us their reverse side but without managing to deceive us.

Against frankness

It is prudent to be equally wary of Percy, Laurence and Augustin. Laurence recites poetry, Percy lectures, and Augustin tells truths. A frank person – that is the latter's title, and his profession is that of being a true friend.

Augustin comes into a salon; verily I tell you, be on your guard and never forget that he is truly your friend. Remember that, just like Percy and Laurence, he never comes with impunity, and that he will not wait for you to ask him before telling you a few truths about yourself, any more than Laurence waited before delivering a monologue before you, or Percy before telling you what he thinks of Verlaine. He does not let you wait for him or interrupt him, since he is frank in the same way as Laurence is a lecturer, not in your interest, but for his own pleasure. To be sure, your displeasure intensifies his pleasure, just as your attention intensifies the pleasure of Laurence. But he could forgo it if necessary. So here we have them, three impudent scoundrels to whom we should refuse all encouragement, all indulgence, and anything, indeed, which feeds their vice. Quite the contrary, for they have their own special audience which they can live off. Indeed, the audience of Augustin the sayer of truths is quite extensive. This audience, misled by the conventional psychology of the theatre and the absurd maxim, 'Who loves well chastises well', refuses to recognise that flattery is sometimes merely an overflow of affection, and frankness the foam and slobber of a bad mood. Does Augustin exercise his spite on a friend? His audience draws a vague mental contrast between Roman rough justice and Byzantine hypocrisy, and they all exclaim with a proud gesture, their eyes lit by jubilation at feeling themselves to be morally better, more down to earth, altogether rougher and tougher, 'He's not someone to spare your feelings out of affection!… Let's honour him: what a true friend!…'

An elegant milieu is one in which the opinion of each consists of the opinion of all the others. And if the opinion of each consists in holding the *opposite* opinion to all the others, it's a literary milieu.

*

The libertine's desire to take a virgin is still a form of the eternal homage paid by love to innocence.

*

On leaving the **, you go to see the ***, and the stupidity, the malice, and the wretched situation of the ** is dissected before your eyes. Overwhelmed by admiration for the lucidity of the ***, you at first blush with shame at having initially had any esteem for the **. But when you go back to see them again, they shoot holes through the *** using more or less the same tactics. To go from one to the other is to visit two enemy camps. But as the one side can never hear the shots fired by the other, it thinks that it alone is armed. Once you have noticed that the supply of arms is the same and that the strength, or rather the weakness, is more or less equal on each side, you cease to admire the side that is shooting and to despise the side under attack. This is the beginning of wisdom. Wisdom itself would mean having nothing more to do with either side.

11

Scenario

Honoré is sitting in his bedroom. He rises and looks at himself in the mirror:

HIS CRAVAT: How many times have you languorously tied my expressive and slightly loose knot, and dreamily patted it into shape? So you are in love, dear friend; but why are you sad?…

HIS PEN: Yes, why are you sad? For a whole week you have been over-working me, master, and yet I have really changed my lifestyle. I, who seemed destined for more glorious tasks, am starting to think that I will never write anything other than love letters, to judge from this writing paper you have just had designed for yourself. But those love letters will be sad – I can foresee as much from the attacks of hysteric-al despair during which you pick me up and put me back straight down again. You are in love, my friend, but why are you sad?…

ROSES, ORCHIDS, HORTENSIAS, MAIDENHAIR FERNS, AND COLUM-BINES [*which fill the bedroom*]: You have always loved us, but never did you summon us in such numbers together to charm you with our proud and winsome poses, our eloquent gestures and the touching intonations of our perfume! To be sure, we represent to you the fresh graces of your beloved. You are in love, but why are you sad?…

BOOKS: We were ever your prudent councillors, always being asked for advice and never heeded. But even if we have never impelled you to act, we did make you understand – and when you nonetheless rushed to your defeat, at least you did not find yourself struggling in the dark, as if in a nightmare: do not relegate us to a distant corner, like old tutors no longer required. You held us in your childish hands. Your eyes, still pure, were filled with astonishment as you contemplated us. If you do not love us for ourselves, love us for the way we remind you about yourself, about all that you have been, all that you might have been; and the fact that you might have been such a person means, does it not, that while you were dreaming of being it, to some extent you *were* it?

Come and hear our familiar, sermonising voice; we will not tell you why you are in love, but we will tell you why you are sad, and if our child is filled with despair and begins to weep, we will tell him stories, we will cradle him as once we did when the voice of his mother lent its sweet authority to our words, in front of the fire flickering with all its flames, and with all your hopes and all your dreams.

HONORÉ: I am in love with her and I think I will be loved in return. But my heart tells me that I, who was once so changeable, will always be in love with her, and my good fairy knows that I will be loved by her for only a month. That is why, before entering the paradise of those brief joys, I halt on the threshold to wipe my eyes.

HIS GOOD FAIRY: Dear friend, I have come from heaven to bring you mercy, and your happiness will depend on you yourself. If, for a month, you are prepared to take the risk of spoiling, by an artificial stratagem, the joys you had promised yourself from this relationship, if you disdain the woman you love, if you contrive to behave with a certain coquetry and pretend to be indifferent to her, not turning up at the meeting place you had arranged and refusing to place your lips on her bosom that she will proffer to you like a bouquet of roses, then your mutual, faithful love will rise up proud and strong for all eternity on the incorruptible foundation of your patience.

HONORÉ [*jumping for joy*]: My good fairy, I adore you and I will obey you!

THE LITTLE DRESDEN CLOCK: Your lady friend is not punctual, my finger has already passed the minute you had been dreaming of for so long, the minute at which your beloved was supposed to arrive. I am fearful of marking time for you, with my monotonous tick-tock, as you languish in melancholy expectation; while I know what time is, I understand nothing of life; sad hours take the place of joyful minutes, and melt together within me like bees in a beehive...

The bell rings; a servant goes to open the door.

THE GOOD FAIRY: Remember to obey me: the eternity of your love depends on it.

The clock ticks feverishly, the perfume of the roses grows disquieted, and the orchids twist and turn towards Honoré in anxious torment; one of them has a malicious expression. His inert pen considers him, filled with sadness at not being able to move. The books do not cease from their grave murmuring. Everything tells him, 'Obey the fairy and remember that the eternity of your love depends on doing so...'

HONORÉ [*without hesitating*]: Of course I will obey! How can you doubt me?

The beloved enters; the roses, the orchids, the maidenhair ferns, the pen and paper, the Dresden clock, and a breathless Honoré all quiver as if vibrating in harmony with her. Honoré flings himself onto her mouth, crying: I love you!...

EPILOGUE: – It was as if he had blown out the flame of the beloved's desire. Pretending to be shocked by the indecent way he had just behaved, she fled, and whenever he encountered her again, it was only to see her torturing him with a stern and indifferent gaze…

1 2

A painted fan

Madame, I have painted this fan for you.

May it, at your desire, evoke in your retreat the vain and charming shapes that peopled your salon, so rich as it then was in gracious living, but now forever closed.

The chandeliers, all of whose branches bear great pale flowers, shed their radiance on objets d'art from every time and from every land. I kept the spirit of our age in mind while, with my paintbrush, I led the curious glances of those chandeliers to the varied range of your bibelots. Like them, that spirit has contemplated examples of the thought or the life of different centuries throughout the world. It has immeasurably extended the circle of its excursions. Out of pleasure, and out of boredom, it has made them as varied as if they were so many different paths down which to stroll, and now, disheartened at not finding its goal, or even the way to it, and feeling its forces fail and its courage abandoning it, it lies flat on its face on the ground so as to see nothing more, like a brute. And yet I painted the rays shed by your chandeliers with such tenderness; they caressed, with an amorous melancholy, so many things and so many people, and now they are extinguished forever. Despite the small dimensions of the frame, you will perhaps recognise the persons in the foreground, and the way the impartial painter has given equal value, as does your evenly distributed affection, to great lords, beautiful women, and men of talent. This was a bold way of reconciling them in the eyes of the world, albeit inadequate and unjust when judged by the tenets of reason, and yet it made of your society a microcosm, less divided and more harmonious than the other universe – a microcosm that was still alive, and that we will never see again. So I would not like my fan to be studied by an indifferent spectator who had never frequented salons such as yours and would be surprised to see 'politeness' bringing together dukes devoid of arrogance and novelists devoid of pretentiousness. But perhaps this stranger would also fail to understand the drawbacks of such a juxta-position, whose excess soon leads to a mere exchange of absurdities. Doubtless he would find a pessimistic realism in the spectacle of the wing chair on the right, where a great author, with all the appearances of a snob, is listening to a great lord who seems to be holding forth on the poem he is leafing through, a poem of which, to judge by the expression in his eyes (if I have managed adequately to depict their inanity), he clearly understands nothing.

Near the fireplace you will recognise C***.

He is unstopping a small bottle and explaining to the woman next to him that he has formed a concentrate of the most potent and most exotic perfumes.

B***, in despair at the fact that he cannot outdo his rival, and reflecting that the surest way of overtaking fashion is to be brazenly old-fashioned, is sniffing two pennyworth of violets and staring contemptuously at C***.

Did not you yourself try to get 'back to nature' by resorting to these artificial means? I would like to have depicted (if such details had not been too tiny to be made out clearly), in a quiet corner of your musical library of that period, your Wagner operas, your symphonies by Franck and d'Indy pushed to one side, and on your piano some scores by Haydn, Handel or Palestrina, all still open.

I had no compunction about depicting you on the pink sofa. T*** is there, sitting next to you. He is describing his new bedroom, skilfully treated with tar to evoke the sensations of a sea journey, and he is detailing for you all the quintessences of his dressing table and his furnishings.

Your disdainful smile bears witness to the fact that you have little esteem for that infirm imagination which finds that a bare bedroom is not in itself quite enough to contain within it all the visions of the universe – an imagination which conceives of art and beauty in such a pitifully materialistic way.

Your most delightful lady friends are there. Would they ever forgive me if you were to show them my fan? I don't know. The most strangely beautiful of them, who seemed a living and breathing Whistler to our marvelling eyes, would not have recognised and admired herself unless she had been portrayed by Bouguereau. Women incarnate beauty without understanding it.

They will say, perhaps, 'We merely like a beauty different from yours. Why should it be any less beautiful?'

Let them allow me at least to say this: how few women understand the aesthetic which makes them what they are! A Botticelli virgin would have found Botticelli himself gauche and artless, were it not for the dictates of fashion.

Accept this fan with indulgence. If one of the shades that, after flitting through my memory, have settled on it, happened – while still a participant in life – to make you weep, then recognise it without bitterness, reflecting that it is a shade and will not make you suffer any more.

I have managed to set down these shades innocently on this frail paper, to which the movement of your hand will give wings, only because they are too unreal and too insignificant to be able to do any harm…

No more harm, perhaps, than when you invited them to come for a few hours to forestall death and live the vain life of phantoms, in the artificial joys of your salon, under the chandeliers whose branches were covered with great pale flowers.

13

Olivian

Why do we see you going to the theatre every evening, Olivian? Don't your friends have more wit than Pantaloon, Scaramouche or Pasquarello? And would it not be nicer to have supper with them? But you could do better. If the theatre is the resort of conversationalists with tongue-tied friends or insipid mistresses, then conversation, however exquisite, is the pleasure of men without imagination. It is a complete waste of time trying to tell you, Olivian, what a man of wit does not need to have dunned into him, since he learns it quite simply by making conversation. The voice of the soul and the imagination is the only voice which can make the entire soul and imagination echo in harmony; and part of the time you killed in trying to make yourself popular would have given you – if only you had brought that time to life, if you had nourished it with reading or reverie, by your fireside in the winter or in your gardens in the summer – a rich memory of deeper and fuller hours. Have the courage to take up your spade and your rake. One day, you will be filled with pleasure when you smell a sweet perfume rising from your memory, as from a wheelbarrow filled to brimming.

Why do you travel so much? Carriages take you so slowly to destinations you could reach so quickly in your dreams. In order to be at the seaside, you need only close your eyes. Let those who have only bodily eyes force their entire households to follow them and settle in Pozzuoli or Naples. You want to finish a book there, you say? Where will you work better than here in town? Within its walls, you can elaborate the most grandiose settings you desire; here you will avoid more easily than in Pozzuoli the lunches given by the Princess of Bergamo, and you will be less often tempted to go for a stroll without accomplishing anything. Above all, why do you insist so strenuously on enjoying the present, weeping when you cannot manage to do so? Man of imagination, you can enjoy things only in nostalgia or in anticipation: in other words, you can enjoy only the past or the future.

That is why, Olivian, you are discontented with your mistress, your holidays in the country, and yourself. The reason for these ills is something that you have perhaps already noted; but in that case, why do you continue to wallow in them rather than trying to be cured of them? The fact is that you are thoroughly wretched, Olivian. You have hardly reached manhood, and already you are a man of letters.

14

Characters from the social comedy

Just as in comedies Scaramouche is always boastful and Harlequin always oafish, the behaviour of Pasquino is plotting and intrigue and that of Pantaloon avarice and credulity; likewise, society has decreed that Guido is witty but treacherous, and would not hesitate to sacrifice a friend for the sake of a clever joke; that Girolamo hoards, beneath an external appearance of rough-and-ready frankness, treasures of sensitivity; that Castruccio, whose vices anyone can castigate, is the most faithful friend and the most scrupulous son; that Iago, despite ten fine books, is a mere amateur, while a few poor newspaper articles have immediately meant that Ercole is acclaimed as a writer; and that Cesare must be something of a policeman – a reporter or a spy. Cardenio is a snob and Pippo's amiability is quite insincere, for all his protestations of friendship. As for Fortunata, the definitive verdict has been pronounced: she is nice and kind. Her plump curves are quite enough to guarantee the benevolence of her character: how could such a fat lady be a nasty person?

In addition, each person is by nature quite different from the character which society has fetched from the general store of roles and costumes and imposed on him once and for all, and deviates all the more from that character since the a-priori conception of his good qualities, by opening up for him a generous credit of the corresponding failings, gives him the benefit of a sort of impunity. His immutable character as a faithful friend in general allows Castruccio to betray each of his friends in particular. Only the friend suffers from it: 'What a villain he must have been for Castruccio – such a faithful friend – to abandon him!' Fortunata can spill rivers of malicious gossip. Who would be foolish enough to seek the source of those rumours within the folds of her bodice, whose shapeless plumpness serves to conceal everything? Girolama can practise flattery without fear, since his habitual frankness makes it seem even more piquantly unexpected. He can treat one of his friends with a rudeness bordering on ferocity, since it is understood that this brutality is all in the friend's best interests.

Cesare asks me about my health: it is so he can report back to the Doge. He didn't even ask me how I am: how well he knows how to hide his hand! Guido comes up to greet me, he compliments me on how well I am looking. 'Nobody is as witty as he is, but he really is too spiteful!' chorus all those present. This divergence between the true characters of Castruccio, Guido, Cardenio, Ercole, Pippo, Cesare and Fortunata, and the type they irrevocably incarnate in the oh-so-wise eyes of society, is quite without danger for them, since society refuses to see this divergence. But this divergence itself has its limits. Whatever Girolama may do, he *is* a rough diamond. Whatever Fortunata may say, she *is* kind. The absurd, massive, unchanging persistence of the type, from which these people may ceaselessly diverge without ever disturbing its serene immutability, ends up by imposing itself on them with an increasing force of attraction: they are people of no great originality and little consistency in behaviour, and they are eventually hypnotised by this fixed identity which alone remains forever the same amidst their universal variations. Girolamo, telling a friend a few 'home truths', is grateful to be able to act as his stooge in this way, and by 'scolding him for his own good', he ensures that his friend allows him to play an honourable, indeed brilliant role – one that is now almost sincere. He tempers the violence of his diatribes with an indulgent pity that is perfectly natural towards an inferior who thereby acts as a foil to his own glory; he is really grateful to him, and is finally filled with the very same cordial affection that people have attributed to him for so long, that he has ended up really feeling it. Fortunata, whose increasing plumpness, without adversely affecting her wit or diminishing her beauty, has somewhat diminished her interest in others the more the sphere of her own personality has expanded, feels a mellowing of the tetchiness that alone prevented her from fulfilling the venerable and charming functions which society had delegated to her. The meaning of the words 'generous', 'kind', and 'big-hearted', ceaselessly uttered in her presence and behind her back, has slowly soaked into her own conversation, in which she now usually expresses a praise on which her vast rotundity confers, as it were, a more flattering authority. She has the vague but deep sense that she is exercising a considerable and pacific magistracy. Sometimes this appears to overflow her own individuality, and then it appears as the plenary assembly, stormy and yet easily swayed, of the benevolent judges over whom she presides and whose assent is her foremost concern... And at those evening gatherings where people are busily conversing, all of them – without finding the inconsistencies in the behaviour of these characters in the slightest problematic, and without noticing how they have gradually adapted to the type imposed on them – carefully tidy away their actions into the correct drawer (neatly labelled and docketed) of their 'ideal characters', and feel with more than a touch of satisfaction that the level of conversation is unquestionably rising. Of course, they soon interrupt this labour so as not to overburden or overstrain heads which are not really in the habit of abstract thought (one *is* a man of the world, after all). Then, after lambasting the snobbery of the one, the spite of the other, and the libertinage or hard-heartedness of a third, they go their separate ways; and each of them, sure of having paid a generous tribute to kindliness, modesty and charity, goes off to indulge – without remorse, in the tranquillity of a clear conscience that has just shown its mettle – in the elegant vices that he practises simultaneously.

These reflections, inspired by the society of Bergamo, would, if applied to a different one, lose much of their truth. When Harlequin left the stage of Bergamo for that of France, he stopped being oafish and became a wit. It is thus that in certain societies Liduvina passes for a superior woman and Girolamo for a man of wit. One should also add that a man sometimes appears for whom society has no ready-made character or at least no character available, since someone else is already playing that role. First, society tries out on him characters that don't suit him. If he really is an original man and no character is worthy of him, society, incapable of resigning itself to trying to understand him, and lacking a character that will fit him, excludes him – unless, that is, he can gracefully play the role of romantic lead, something we can never have enough of.

BOUVARD AND PÉCUCHET
ON SOCIETY AND MUSIC

1

*Society**

'Now that we have a position,' said Bouvard, 'why shouldn't we go out into society like everyone else?'

This was also Pécuchet's view; but they would need to shine in society, and to do that, they should study the subjects which people talk about.

Contemporary literature is of the highest importance.

They took out a subscription to the various journals which publish contemporary literature; they read them aloud, and endeavoured to write reviews, seeking above all a light and fluent style, in view of the aim they had set themselves.

Bouvard objected that the style of literary criticism, even when it is written in a light-hearted tone, does not suit social gatherings. And they practised making conversation about what they had read in the manner of society people.

Bouvard would lean against the fireplace, and fiddle cautiously – so as not to get them dirty – with a pair of buff-coloured gloves brought out expressly for the occasion, addressing Pécuchet as 'Madame' or 'General', so as to make the illusion complete.

But often, this was as far as they would get; or, when one of them started to wax enthusiastic about an author, the other would try in vain in stop him. In any case, they disparaged everything. Leconte de Lisle was too devoid of passion, Verlaine was too sensitive. They dreamt of a golden mean, but never found it.

'Why does Loti always sound the same?'

'His novels always follow the same old tune.'

'He has only one string to his bow,' concluded Bouvard.

'But André Laurie isn't any more satisfying – every year he takes us

* The opinions ascribed here to the two celebrated characters from Flaubert are, of course, in no way those of the author.[3]

off to a different place and confuses literature with geography. It's only his style that makes it any good. As for Henri de Régnier, he's a charlatan or a madman, there are no two ways about it.'

'If you can get beyond that, old fellow,' said Bouvard, 'you'll help contemporary literature to escape from the dreadful dead end it's reached.'

'Why force them?' said Pécuchet in lordly but avuncular tones. 'Perhaps those young colts have some spunk in them. Let's give them free rein; the only danger is that they might be so hot-blooded that they overshoot the mark; but such extravagance is in itself the proof of a rich nature.'

'And meanwhile, barriers will be broken down!' cried Pécuchet; and filling the echoing room with his counter-arguments, he became heated: 'And you can keep telling me till you're blue in the face that these unequal lines are poetry: I refuse to see anything other than prose in them, and meaningless prose at that!'

Mallarmé is no more talented than the rest, but he's a brilliant conversationalist. What a misfortune it is that such a gifted man should go quite mad each time he picks up his pen. This is a singular malady, and it seemed to them quite inexplicable. Maeterlinck can shock, but he uses material means that are unworthy of the theatre; his art affects you as powerfully as a crime, it's horrible! Anyway, his syntax is awful.

They conducted a spirited critique of his style, parodying his dialogue in the form of a conjugation:

'I said the woman had come in.'

'You said the woman had come in.'

'We said the woman had come in.'

'Why did they say that the woman had come in?'

Pécuchet wanted to send this little piece to *La Revue des Deux Mondes*, but it would be a better idea, countered Bouvard, to keep it to themselves and then trot it out in some fashionable salon. They would be immediately judged on their merits. They could easily send it to a review later. And the first beneficiaries of this witty sally, on reading it subsequently, would be retrospectively flattered at having attended its premiere.

Lemaitre, for all his wit, struck them as inconsequential, irreverent, sometimes pedantic and sometimes bourgeois; he kept withdrawing his views. His style in particular was too lax, but the difficulty of improvising to strict and frequent deadlines could serve to excuse him. As for France, he is a good writer, but a poor thinker, as opposed to Bourget, who is deep, but has a dismal sense of form. The scarcity of an all-round talent filled them with melancholy.

But it shouldn't be all that difficult – Bouvard would reflect – to express your ideas clearly. But clarity is not enough: you need grace (combined with force), vivacity, elevation, and logic. And irony too, added Bouvard. But according to Pécuchet, irony is not indispensable; it is often wearisome, and it is an unnecessary complication for the reader. In short, everybody writes badly. The fault lay, according to Bouvard, in an excessive quest for originality; and according to Pécuchet, in the decadence of contemporary life.

'Let us be brave enough to keep our conclusions to ourselves in social circles,' said Bouvard; 'we would appear as carping critics and, by alarming everyone, we would displease them all. Let us provide reassurance rather than anxiety. Our originality will be enough of a drawback for us as it is. We should even try to conceal it. We don't *have* to talk about literature.'

But other things really are important.

'How should you bow to someone? With your whole body or just your head, slowly or quickly, as you are standing or clicking your heels together, moving closer or staying put, tucking in your lower back or transforming it into a pivot? Should your hands hang down your sides, or hold onto your hat, or wear gloves? Should your face remain serious or smile throughout the duration of your bow? But how can one immediately resume one's gravity once one has finished bowing?'

Introducing someone is difficult too.

Whose name should you begin with? Should you indicate the person you are naming with a wave of the hand, or a nod of the head, or should you remain motionless and look indifferent? Should you bow in the same way to an old man and a young man, a locksmith and a prince, an actor and an academician? An affirmative response satisfied Pécuchet's egalitarian ideas, but shocked Bouvard's common sense.

How could you give everyone their correct title?

You say 'hello' to a baron, a viscount, and a count; but 'hello, my lord' seemed to them too pedestrian, and 'hello, marquess' too cavalier, given their age. So they resigned themselves to saying 'prince' to a prince and 'my lord' to a duke, even though this latter usage struck them as revolting. When they got as far as the Highnesses, they became perplexed; Bouvard, flattered at the idea of his future acquaintances, imagined a thousand sentences in which this form of address appeared in every shape and size; he would accompany it with a bashful little smile, bowing his head slightly, and hopping from foot to foot. But Pécuchet declared that he'd get confused and keep muddling them up, or would burst out laughing in the prince's face. In short, to simplify things, they just wouldn't go into the *faubourg* Saint-Germain. But the *faubourg* extends everywhere, and only from a distance does it look like a compact and isolated whole!... In any case, titles are even more respected in the upper echelons of the banking world, and as for the titles of foreign parvenus, you just can't keep count of them. But in Pécuchet's view, you should be intransigent when it came to fake nobles, and make a point of not giving them their full titles, even on the envelopes of letters or when talking to their servants. Bouvard, more of a sceptic, saw their obsession with titles as merely a more recent fad, but one just as respectable as that of the great lords of old. In any case, in their opinion, the nobility had ceased to exist ever since it had lost its privileges. The nobility supports the clergy, is backward, doesn't read books, does nothing, just has a good time as much as does the bourgeoisie; they found it absurd to respect it. It was only possible to frequent it because you could still express your contempt while doing so. Bouvard declared that in order to know where they would pay their social calls, to which suburbs they would venture once a year, and where the arenas of their habits and vices would be located, they first of all needed to draw up an exact plan of Parisian society. It included, in his view, the *faubourg* Saint-Germain, the world of finance, that of foreign parvenus, Protestant society, the world of the arts and the theatre, and the official and scholarly world. The *faubourg*, in Pécuchet's view, concealed beneath its rigid exterior all the libertinage of the Ancien Régime. Every noble has mistresses and a sister who is a nun, and conspires with the clergy. They are brave, run up debts, ruin and abuse moneylenders, and are inevitably the champions of honour. They reign through their elegance, invent extravagant fashions, are exemplary sons, affectionate towards the common people, and hard on bankers. They always have a sword in their hand, or a woman riding behind them; they dream of the restoration of the monarchy, and are dreadfully lazy, but not haughty with ordinary folk; they cause traitors to flee and they insult cowards, and they deserve, thanks to a certain chivalric aura, our unwavering affection.

On the other hand, high finance, dignified and dour, inspires respect but also aversion. The financier is consumed by worries even at the wildest ball. One of his countless clerks is always turning up to bring him the latest news from the Stock Exchange, even at four in the morning; he hides his greatest triumphs and his worst disasters from his wife. No one even knows if he is a potentate or a crook; he is both of them in turn, quite unpredictably, and in spite of his vast fortune, he pitilessly throws out his small tenant when the latter gets behind with his rent, not even giving him an extension unless he wants to use him as a spy or sleep with his daughter. In any case, he is always in his carriage, dresses without elegance, and habitually wears a pince-nez.

They did not feel any more warmly towards Protestant society; it is frigid, stuck-up, gives money only to its own poor, and is exclusively composed of pastors. Protestant churches look too much like their homes, and their homes are as gloomy as their churches. They always have a pastor round for lunch; the servants remonstrate with their masters by quoting chapter and verse from the Bible; they are too afraid of gaiety to have anything to hide and when conversing with Catholics they keep alluding to their perpetual grudge over the Revocation of the Edict of Nantes and the Massacre of St Bartholomew.

The world of the arts, while just as homogeneous, is quite different; every artist is a practical joker who has quarrelled with his family, never wears a top hat, and speaks a special language. They spend their lives dodging the bailiffs who come to distrain their goods, and inventing grotesque disguises for masked balls. Nonetheless, they produce a constant stream of masterpieces, and for most of them the abuse of alcohol and women is the very condition of their inspiration, if not of their genius; they sleep during the day, go out for a walk at night, work heaven knows when, with their heads thrown back, letting their loosely knotted cravats float in the wind while they perpetually roll cigarettes.

The world of the theatre is hardly distinguishable from the world of artists; family life is never paid its proper respect; theatre people are eccentric and inexhaustibly generous. Actors, despite being vain and jealous, always help out their comrades, applaud their successes, adopt the children of actresses suffering from tuberculosis or misfortune, and are inclined to be affected in society even though, never having received any education, they are often devout and always superstitious. Those who work in the subsidised theatres are a case apart, entirely worthy of our admiration, and they would deserve to be seated at table before a general or a prince; their souls are filled with the sentiments expressed in the masterpieces they perform in our great playhouses. Their memories are prodigious and they are always immaculately turned out.

As for the Jews, Bouvard and Pécuchet, without entirely proscribing them (you have to be a liberal, after all), admitted that they hated finding themselves in their company; they had all sold pince-nez in Germany in their youth, and even in Paris they insisted on preserving – with a piety which, as impartial spectators, our heroes handsomely acknowledged – special practices, an unintelligible vocabulary, and butchers from their own race. They all have hooked noses, an exceptional intelligence, and base souls intent only on seeking their own advantage; their women, on the other hand, are beautiful, a little on the flabby side, but capable of the deepest feelings. How many Catholics ought to imitate them! But why are their fortunes always incalculable and hidden? In addition, they formed a sort of vast secret society, like the Jesuits and the Freemasons. They had inexhaustible treasures stowed away, nobody knew where, at the service of unspecified enemies, always available for some terrible and mysterious purpose.

2

Music

Already tired of cycling and painting, Bouvard and Pécuchet set out to make a serious study of music. But whereas Pécuchet, that eternal friend of tradition and order, allowed himself to be hailed as the last devotee of bawdy songs and the *Domino noir*[4], Bouvard, a revolutionary if ever there was one, showed himself to be, we have to confess, 'a staunch Wagnerian'. In point of fact, he did not know a single score by the 'Berlin bawler' (as Pécuchet, always patriotic and ill-informed, cruelly nicknamed him), since they could not be heard in France, where the Conservatory stagnates in its routine, between Colonne who stammers and Lamoureux who stutters,[5] nor in Munich, where the tradition has not been preserved, nor in Bayreuth, which has been overrun by snobs to an intolerable degree. It's nonsensical to try and play them on the piano: the illusion of the stage is necessary, as is putting the orchestra in a buried pit and insisting on darkness in the auditorium. However, always on view to make visitors reel with surprise, the prelude to *Parsifal* lay permanently open on the music stand of his piano, between the photographs of César Franck's penholder and the *Primavera* of Botticelli.

From the score of *The Valkyrie*, the 'spring scene' had been carefully ripped out. In the table of contents of Wagner's operas, on the first page, an indignant stroke of red pencil had struck out *Lohengrin* and *Tannhäuser*. *Rienzi* alone of the first operas still survived. To deny its merits was commonplace, and the time had come – Bouvard sensed with his subtle flair – to start promoting the opposite view. Gounod made him laugh, and Verdi made him scream. He was less good, admittedly, than Erik Satie – who could deny it? Beethoven, however, seemed to him as considerable a figure as some Messiah. Bouvard himself could, without undue false modesty, salute Bach as a precursor. Saint-Saëns has no content and Massenet no form, he kept saying to Pécuchet, in whose eyes, on the contrary, Saint-Saëns was all content and Massenet all form.

'That's the reason why the one educates us and the other delights us, but without elevating us,' insisted Pécuchet.

For Bouvard, both of them were equally contemptible. Massenet could come up with a few ideas, but they were vulgar ones – anyway, we've had quite enough of ideas. Saint-Saëns had some sense of shape, but it was old-fashioned. They did not know very much about Gaston Lemaire, but they enjoyed making comparisons from time to time, and so they eloquently contrasted Chausson with Chaminade. Pécuchet, in any case, despite the reticence dictated by his aesthetic code, and even Bouvard himself (for every Frenchman is chivalrous and always puts women first) gallantly awarded to the latter the first place among the composers of the day.

In Bouvard, it was the democrat even more than the musician who condemned the music of Charles Levadé; lingering over the poetry of Mme de Girardin in the century of steam, universal suffrage and the bicycle is surely tantamount to opposing progress? In any case, since he was a proponent of art for art's sake, of playing without nuance and singing without inflexion, Bouvard declared that he could not bear to hear him sing. He found that he looked like a musketeer, with mockingly flamboyant manners and the facile elegance of a superannuated sentimentality.

But the subject of their liveliest debates was Reynaldo Hahn. While his close friendship with Massenet, bringing the cruel and unremitting sarcasm of Bouvard down on his head, also marked him out as a prey to the passionate predilections of Pécuchet, he nonetheless contrived to exasperate the latter through his admiration for Verlaine, an admiration which Bouvard shared. 'Set Jacques Normand to music, or Sully Prudhomme, or the Vicomte de Borelli! Thank God, in the land of the troubadours, there is no lack of poets,' he would add patriotically. And, torn between the Teutonic sonorities of the name of Hahn and the southern ending of his first name Reynaldo, preferring to condemn him out of hatred for Wagner rather than to absolve him because of Verdi, he would conclude, with perfect logic, as he turned to Bouvard:

'Despite the effort of all your fine gentlemen, our lovely land of France is a land of clarity, and French music will be clear or will not be at all,' whereupon he emphasised his verdict by banging on the table to give extra force to his words.

'I pour scorn on your eccentricities from beyond the English Channel and your mists from beyond the Rhine – stop looking to the other side of the Vosges!' he added, gazing at Bouvard with a stern and fixed expression filled with unspoken implications – 'unless it is for the defence of our fatherland! That the *Valkyrie* can ever give pleasure even in Germany, I very much doubt… But for French ears, it will always be the most infernal torment – and the most cacophonous, not to say the most humiliating for our national pride! Anyway, doesn't that opera combine the most revolting kind of incest with the most atrocious forms of dissonance? Your music, Monsieur, is full of monsters, and you never know what people will dream up next! Even in nature – even though she is the mother of simplicity – only what is horrible gives you any pleasure. Doesn't Monsieur Delafosse write songs about bats, in which the composer's extravagance is bound to compromise the pianist's long-standing reputation? Why couldn't he choose some nice little bird? Songs about sparrows would at least be perfectly Parisian; the swallow has lightness and grace, and the lark is so thoroughly French that Caesar, they say, had his soldiers roast them and stick them on their helmets. But bats!!! The French, always athirst for openness and clarity, will always detest that animal of darkness. In the poetry of Monsieur de Montesquiou, maybe… we can just about allow him that: it's the whim of a rather blasé *grand seigneur* – but in music! It won't be long before someone writes a *Requiem for Kangaroos*!…' This jest smoothed the wrinkles from Bouvard's brow.

'Admit that I've made you laugh,' said Pécuchet (without any reprehensible fatuousness – we can allow men of wit a certain awareness of their own merits). 'Let's shake on it: you are quite disarmed!'

MME DE BREYVES'S MELANCHOLY
SUMMER VACATION

Ariadne, my sister, pierced by what love
Did you die on the shores where you were abandoned?[6]

1

Françoise de Breyves hesitated for a long time, that evening, before deciding whether to go to the reception at the home of Princess Elisabeth of A***, to the opera, or to the Livrays' play.

At the friends' house where she had just dined, everyone had left table over an hour ago. She had to make up her mind.

Her friend Geneviève, who was meant to be returning with her, was plumping for the reception at the home of Mme d'A***, whereas, without altogether knowing why, Mme de Breyves would have preferred one of the other two options, or even a third: going home to bed. Her carriage was announced. She still hadn't reached a decision.

'Really,' said Geneviève, 'it's not very nice of you – I think Rezké is going to sing and I enjoy that. Anyone would think it would have serious consequences for you if you went to Elisabeth's. For one thing, you know, you haven't been to a single one of her big receptions this year, and since you're so close to her, that's not very nice of you.'

Ever since the death of her husband, which had left her – four years ago – a widow at the age of twenty, Françoise hardly ever did anything without Geneviève, and liked to please her. She put up no further resistance to her request, and after bidding farewell to her hosts and the other guests, who were all sorry to have had so little chance to enjoy the company of one of the most sought-after women in Paris, she said to the footman:

'Take me to the home of the Princess of A***.'

The evening at the Princess's was extremely boring. At one moment Mme de Breyves asked Geneviève:

'So who's that young man who took you over to the buffet?'

'That's Monsieur de Laléande, whom I don't know at all, actually. Do you want me to introduce him? He'd asked me to, but I didn't give a definite reply, as he's quite insignificant and boring – and since he thinks you're very pretty, he'd never let go of you.'

'Oh, in that case, no!' said Françoise, 'he's rather plain, actually, and rather commonplace, though he does have quite nice eyes.'

'You're right,' said Geneviève. 'And anyway, you'll be meeting him quite often, it might be awkward for you if you knew him.'

And she added, jokingly, 'Though if you *would* like to get to know him on a more intimate footing, you're wasting a very fine opportunity.'

'Yes, a very fine opportunity,' said Françoise – and her mind was already on something else.

'After all,' said Geneviève, no doubt overcome by remorse at having been such an unfaithful go-between, and having deprived that young man of a little pleasure for no reason at all, 'this is one of the last receptions of the season, it wouldn't be really serious and it might perhaps be nicer of you.'

'Oh all right then, if he comes back over this way.'

He did not come over. He was at the other end of the salon, opposite them.

'We have to go,' Geneviève said shortly.

'Just another few minutes,' said Françoise.

And on a whim, above all out of a certain desire to flirt with that young man, who must indeed find her very pretty, she started to fix a lingering gaze on him, then looked away, only to gaze at him again. As she stared at him, she did her best to adopt a caressing manner, she didn't know why – for no particular reason, for the pleasure of it, the pleasure of charity, and to some extent the pleasure of pride, and the pleasure of doing something useless, the pleasure of those who write a name on a tree for some passer-by whom they will never see, or those who cast a bottle into the waves. Time was passing, it was already late;

M. de Laléande headed towards the door, which remained open after he had gone out, and Mme de Breyves could see him at the far end of the entrance hall, handing his number to the cloakroom attendant.

'It's time to go, you're quite right,' she said to Geneviève.

They rose to their feet. But as chance would have it, a friend of Geneviève needed to have a word with her, leaving Françoise alone by the cloakroom. The only other person there just then was M. de Laléande, who couldn't find his walking stick. Françoise allowed her gaze to linger on him one last time. He walked by her, lightly brushed Françoise's elbow with his own, and, his eyes shining, said as he bumped into her, seemingly still looking for his stick, 'Come to my place: 5, rue Royale.'

This was so unexpected, and M. de Laléande was already so assiduously looking for his walking stick, that subsequently she was never entirely sure if it hadn't been a hallucination. Above all, she felt very afraid, and as the Prince of A*** was passing by just then, she called him over, and said she wanted to make arrangements for an excursion with him the following day, speaking with great volubility. During this conversation, M. de Laléande had gone. After a while, Geneviève came up and the two women left. Mme de Breyves said nothing of what had happened and remained shocked and flattered, though at bottom quite indifferent. After two days, when by chance she thought back on the incident, she started to doubt the reality of M. de Laléande's words. When she tried to recall them, she was unable to do so fully; she thought that she had heard them as if in a dream, and told herself that the movement he had made with his elbow had just been an accidental moment of clumsiness. Then she quite stopped thinking spontaneously of M. de Laléande, and when by chance she heard someone saying his name, she fleetingly remembered his face but had altogether forgotten the almost hallucinatory encounter by the cloakroom.

She saw him again at the last evening reception to be given that year (it was towards the end of June), though she did not dare ask for him to be introduced to her; and yet, despite finding him almost ugly, and aware of his lack of intelligence, she would really have liked to get to know him. She went up to Geneviève and said to her:

'You may as well introduce me to Monsieur de Laléande. I don't like to be impolite. But don't tell him it was I who asked. That would put the onus on me.'

'I'll do it a bit later if we see him, he isn't here just now.'

'Well, look for him.'

'He may have gone.'

'No,' said Françoise very quickly, 'he can't have gone, it's too early. Oh, midnight already! Come on, Geneviève my dear, it's not all that difficult, you know. The other evening it was you who wanted to. Please do it, I'm really keen.'

Geneviève looked at her in some astonishment and went looking for M. de Laléande; he had already left.

'You see, I was right,' said Geneviève, returning to Françoise.

'I'm dying of boredom here,' said Françoise, 'I've got a headache; please, let's leave right now.'

3

Françoise didn't miss the opera once, and, filled with vague feelings of hope, accepted every invitation to dinner. A fortnight went by, she had not seen M. de Laléande again and often woke up in the middle of the night thinking by what means she might see him. Although she continued to tell herself repeatedly that he was boring and not handsome, she was more preoccupied by him than by all the wittiest and most charming men. Once the season had finished, there would be no further opportunity of seeing him again; she was resolved to create one and kept mulling over the possibilities.

One evening, she said to Geneviève:

'Didn't you tell me that you knew a certain Monsieur de Laléande?'

'Jacques de Laléande? Yes and no – he's been introduced to me, but he has never left his calling card, and I'm not at all well acquainted with him.'

'The fact is, I'll tell you, well, I have some small or maybe even great interest in seeing him and getting to know him, for reasons that don't personally concern me and that I can't disclose to you for a month.'

(Between now and then she would have agreed with him on some lie, so that she wouldn't be caught out; and this thought of a secret known only to the two of them gave her a warm feeling inside.) 'Please, try to find some way of doing this for me – the season is over and nothing will be happening, and I won't be able to have him introduced to me.'

The close practices of friendship, so purifying when they are sincere, protected Geneviève as well as Françoise from the stupid curiosity that is such a vile and intense pleasure for most people in society. And so, with all her heart, without having entertained for a single moment the intention or the desire, or even the idea, of questioning her friend, Geneviève tried to think of a way, and only got cross when she couldn't find one.

'It's such a pity that Madame d'A*** has left. There's Monsieur de Grumello, of course, but actually that won't get us very far – what would we say to him? Ah, I've got an idea! Monsieur de Laléande plays the cello – rather badly, but never mind that. Monsieur de Grumello admires him, and then he's so stupid and will be all too happy to please you. The only problem is, you've always given him the cold shoulder and you don't like just dropping people after you've used them, but you'd then be obliged to invite him next year.'

But already Françoise, flushed with joy, was exclaiming:

'But I don't mind that in the least, I'll invite all the foreign parvenus in Paris if need be! Oh, hurry up and do it, Geneviève my dear, how kind you are!'

And Geneviève wrote:

> *Monsieur, you know how I seek every opportunity to give pleasure to my friend, Mme de Breyves, whom you have doubtless already met. She has several times expressed to me, as we were talking about the cello, how much she regretted never having heard M. de Laléande, who is such a good friend of yours. Would you ask him to play for her and for me? Now that we all have so much time, it will not be too much of an inconvenience for you, and it would be so very kind. With my very best wishes,*
>
> *Alériouvre Buivres*

'Take this note straight away to Monsieur de Grumello's,' said Françoise to a servant; 'don't wait for a reply, but make sure you personally see it is handed in.'

The next day, Geneviève sent Mme de Breyves the following reply from M. de Grumello:

Madame,

I would have been more delighted than you can imagine to satisfy your desire and the wishes of Mme de Breyves, whom I know slightly and for whom I have the warmest and most respectful feelings of friendship. And so I am very sorry indeed to have to tell you that as ill luck would have it, M. de Laléande left just two days ago for Biarritz where, alas! he will be spending several months.

Please accept, Madame, etc.

Grumello

Françoise, white-faced, rushed over to lock her door, and no sooner had she done so than choking sobs were pouring from her lips, and a flood of tears from her eyes. Up until then she had been busy imagining scenarios in which she would meet him and get to know him, sure of being able to turn them into a reality as soon as she wanted: she had lived off this desire and this hope, perhaps without properly realising it. But through a thousand imperceptible roots striking down into all her least conscious moments of happiness or melancholy, filling them with a new sap from an unknown source, this desire had implanted itself in her. Now it was being ripped out of her and cast aside as something impossible. She felt all torn apart: the suffering she felt, as this whole 'herself' was so abruptly uprooted, was appalling, and now that her hopes had suddenly been exposed as baseless and she was plunged into a profound grief, she saw the reality of her love.

4

Françoise withdrew more and more each day from all of life's joys. Even the most intense of them – the ones that she enjoyed in her close relations with her mother or Geneviève, in her hours of music, reading or walking – she experienced distractedly, now that her heart was in the grip of a jealous sorrow that never left her for a single moment. She suffered agonies, both because of the impossibility of going to Biarritz, and also – even if such a thing had been possible – because of her absolute determination *not* to go there and thus compromise, by her unreasonable behaviour, all the prestige she might have in the eyes of M. de Laléande: and her pain was immeasurable. Poor young woman, a victim tortured without knowing why, she was terrified at the thought that this pain would perhaps linger on like this for months before any remedy came, never letting her sleep calmly or dream freely. She was filled with anxiety, too, because she didn't know whether he might pass through Paris – any day now, perhaps – without her knowing. And the fear of letting a happiness that was so close escape her a second time emboldened her; she sent a servant to enquire about M. de Laléande from his concierge. He knew nothing. Then, realising that a sail of hope would never again appear on the sea of grief that spread out to infinity, beyond the horizon of which it seemed there was nothing more, since the world there came to an end, she sensed that she was going to do something crazy, she didn't know what, write to him perhaps – and, acting as her own doctor, so as to calm herself down a bit, she allowed herself to try and let him know that she had been wanting to see him, and she wrote this note to M. de Grumello:

Monsieur,
Mme de Buivres forwarded your kind words to me. I cannot say how grateful and touched I was! But one thing worries me. M. de Laléande did not, I hope, find me indiscreet? If you do not happen to know, ask him and tell me the whole truth, as soon as you have found out. I am filled with curiosity to know, and you will be doing me a real favour. Thank you again, Monsieur.

With my best wishes,
Voragynes Breyves

One hour later, a servant brought her this letter:

You have no cause for concern, Madame. M. de Laléande was quite
unaware that you wished to hear him play. I had asked him which
days he might be able to come and perform at my place, without
saying for whom he would be playing. He replied to me from
Biarritz that he would not be returning before January. And please
do not bother to thank me. You do me the greatest favour by asking
me to do a small one for you, etc.

Grumello

There was nothing else to be done. She did nothing else, fell into an
increasing depression, and was filled with remorse at feeling so sad and
thereby causing her mother sadness. She went to spend a few days in
the country, then left for Trouville. There she heard talk of the social
ambitions of M. de Laléande, and when a prince, striving to please her,
asked, 'Is there any favour I could do for you?' she almost cheered up
on imagining how surprised he would be if she gave him a straight
answer to his question; and she distilled, so as to savour it the more, all
the intoxicating bitterness that she felt in the contrast between all the
great and difficult things people had always done to please her, and this
one small thing, so easy and yet so impossible, that would have restored
her calm, her health, her happiness, and the happiness of her family.
She found a certain enjoyment only in the company of her servants,
who had an immense admiration for her and who served her without
daring to speak to her, sensing how sad she was. Their respectful and
sorrowful silence spoke to her of M. de Laléande. She listened to it with
deep pleasure and made them serve her breakfast very slowly, to defer
the time when her friends would come round and she would need to
put on an act. She wanted to preserve the bittersweet taste of all the
sadness that hung around her because of him, and savour it lingeringly
in her mouth. Even more, she would have liked other people to be
dominated by him too, and found relief in the thought that what
occupied such a large place in her heart filled up a considerable space
around her as well; she would have liked to possess strong and healthy
wild animals who would languish on seeing her pain. At times, in
despair, she wanted to write to him, or get someone else to do so – to
dishonour herself, saying 'nothing really mattered any more'. But it was

better for her, in the very interests of her love, to maintain her social situation, which one day might give her more authority over him – if that day ever came. And should a brief closer acquaintance with him break the spell that he had cast over her (she would not and could not believe it, or even for a single moment imagine it; but her mind, more perspicacious, *could* perceive that cruel and fateful possibility despite the blindness of her heart), she would thereafter remain without a single comfort in the world. And if some other love chanced to come along, she would no longer have the resources that she could at least still count on now – her great influence, which would, on her return to Paris, make it so easy for her to get to know M. de Laléande. Trying to distance herself from her own feelings and examine them objectively, she kept telling herself, 'I know he's nothing special; I've always thought as much. That's my settled opinion of him, and it hasn't wavered. The emotional turmoil set in later, but it has left that first opinion quite unaffected. He's nothing much, but it's for that nothing much that I live. I live for Jacques de Laléande!' But immediately, having uttered his name, by an association of ideas that this time was quite involuntary and irrational, she saw him again, and felt so much euphoria and so much suffering that she sensed that even if he *was* nothing much, that did not matter – he still made her experience sufferings and joys next to which all the rest were as nothing. And even though she reflected that, if she got to know him better, it would all evaporate, she endowed this mirage with all of her pain and all of her longing. A passage from the *Mastersingers* that she had heard at the reception of the Princess of A*** had the capacity to evoke M. de Laléande for her with the greatest precision (*Dem Vogel der heut sang dem war der Schnabel hold gewachsen*[7]). She had involuntarily turned it into the real leitmotif of M. de Laléande and, hearing it one day in a concert in Trouville, she burst into tears. From time to time, not too often in case she started to weary of it, she would shut herself away in her room, where she had had the piano brought in, and started to play it, closing her eyes the better to see him: this was her only joy, an intoxication which left an aftertaste of disenchantment, the opium which she could not do without. Stopping sometimes to listen to the flow of her pain, in the same way that one bends over to hear the sweet incessant plaint of a spring, and thinking of the agonising alternative between her future shame and the subsequent despair of her family on the one hand, and (if she did not yield to her desires) her eternal sadness on the other, she cursed herself for having created such an ingenious balance between the ingredients of pleasure and pain in her love that she had been unable either to reject it at once as a deadly poison, or to cure herself of it. She cursed her eyes first and foremost, and perhaps even more than them her hateful spirit of coquetry and curiosity which had made those eyes open as wide as flowers to tempt that young man, and had then exposed her to the gaze of M. de Laléande, as swift and sure as arrows and more invincible in their sweetness than if they had been injections of morphine. She cursed her imagination too; it had so tenderly nourished her love that Françoise sometimes wandered whether her imagination alone had given birth to it – that love which had now overpowered its mother and was torturing her to death. She cursed her ingenuity as well, which had so skilfully, for good and ill, contrived so many scenarios in which she would be able to see him again, that their frustrating impossibility had perhaps bound her even more tightly to their hero. She cursed her kindness and the delicacy of her heart which, if she were to give herself to him, would infect with remorse and shame the joy of that guilty love; she cursed her impetuous will, rearing up so high and bold to leap over every obstacle every time her desires led it towards an impossible goal, but so weak, so flabby and so broken, not only when she was forced to disobey those desires, but when some other emotion directed her. Finally she cursed her powers of thought, in their divinest aspects – thought, the greatest gift ever granted her; thought, which people have called by every name without ever finding the right one: the poet's intuition, the believer's ecstasy, the profound sense for nature and music; thought, which had placed high peaks and endless horizons before her love, bathing them in the supernatural glow of its allure and in exchange imbuing her love with some of itself; thought, which had taken an interest in this love, shown solidarity with it, and saturated it with its own highest and most intimate inner life, dedicating to it, in the way the treasure in a church is dedicated to the Madonna, all the most precious jewels of her mind and heart – that heart which she could hear lamenting in the evenings, or hovering over the sea whose melancholy was now the sister of the sadness she experienced at not being able to see him. And she cursed that inexpressible sense of the mystery of things, when our minds sink into a radiant beauty, like the sun setting in the sea, for having turned her love into something deeper and more immaterial, more extensive and so to speak infinite, without having made it any less torturing – 'for' (as Baudelaire put it in his evocation of late autumn afternoons), 'there are sensations that, however vague, are still intense, and there is nothing more keenly penetrating than infinity.'

5

autoth' ep' aionos taketaketo phukioessas ex aous, ekhthiston ekhôn hupokardion helkos, Kupridos ek megalas to hoi hêpati pâxe belemnon.

and as soon as the sun rose, he was consumed, there on the seaweed of the shore, keeping in the depths of his heart, like an arrow in his liver, the smarting wound of great Kypris.
(Theocritus, *The Cyclops*)[8]

It is in Trouville that I have just met Mme de Breyves again. I must say I've seen her looking happier than she is now. Nothing can cure her. If she loved M. de Laléande for his good looks or his wit, we could find some wittier or more handsome young man to take her mind off him. If it were his kindness or his love for her that had bound her to him, another man might try to love her with even greater fidelity. But M. de Laléande is neither handsome nor intelligent. He has had no opportunity to prove to her whether he is affectionate or hard-hearted, forgetful or faithful. So it must be he whom she loves, and not certain merits or charms that might be found to an equally high degree in others; it must be he whom she loves, for all his imperfections, all his lack of distinction; she is thus destined to love him in spite of everything. *He* – did she know what this was? All she had to go on was the fact that he filled her, from afar, with such shudders of desolation or bliss that all the rest of her life, everything else in the world, no longer counted for her. The most handsome face, the most original intelligence, would never possess that particular and mysterious essence, so unique that no human being will ever have an exact double even given an infinity of worlds and an eternity of time. Without Geneviève de Buivres, who quite innocently took her to the reception at the home of Mme d'A***, none of this would have happened. But the circumstances joined up to form a chain and imprisoned her, making her the victim of a malady that is incurable because it has no rational explanation. To be sure, M. de Laléande, who is doubtless at this very moment strolling along the beach at Biarritz, leading his mediocre little life filled with footling little dreams, would be quite astonished if he knew of that other life, so miraculously intense that it subordinates everything to itself and annihilates everything apart from itself – the life he leads in the soul of Mme de Breyves, and which is as continuous as his personal life, translating itself just as effectively into acts, and distinguishing itself from his own real life only by a heightened awareness, one less intermittent and more varied. How amazed he would be if he only knew that he, not usually much sought after in his material incarnation, will suddenly appear in her mind's eye wherever she goes, in the company of more talented people, in the most exclusive salons, and amid the most richly satisfying landscapes; and if he only knew that this woman, widely loved as she is, then allows her tenderness, her thoughts, and her attention to focus on the memory of this intruder and on him alone. Everything fades in comparison with him, as if he alone had the reality of a person and as if the other people present were as insubstantial as memories and shadows.

Whether Mme de Breyves is out walking with a poet or lunching at the home of an archduchess, whether she leaves Trouville for the mountains or for the countryside, whether she is alone reading or conversing with the best-loved of her friends, whether she goes out horse riding or drifts off to sleep, the name and the image of M. de Laléande hover over her, delightfully, cruelly, unavoidably, in the same way that the sky hovers over our heads. Things have gone so far that she, who used to hate Biarritz, now finds that everything to do with that town affects her with a painful and unsettling charm. She is anxious to know who is going there – people who will perhaps see him, who will perhaps live with him without appreciating their privilege. For those people she is without rancour, and without daring to ask them to carry out any errands for her, she keeps asking them questions, and is sometimes astonished that they can hear her talking so much about things indirectly connected with her secret, and still not guess it. A large photograph of Biarritz is one of the few decorations in her room. She has given one of the people out for a stroll visible on this photograph, whose face is quite indistinct, the features of M. de Laléande. If only she knew the horrid music he likes and plays, those despised romances would doubtless usurp, first on her piano and before long in her heart, the place of the symphonies of Beethoven or the dramas of Wagner, because of the sentimental dumbing down of her taste, and the charm that the man who is the source of all charm and all pain would project onto them. Sometimes the image of the man she has seen only two or three times, for just a few minutes, the man who holds such a small place in the external events of her life and who has assumed one in her mind and her heart that is so all-absorbing as to fill them entirely – sometimes this image grows faint before the tired eyes of her memory. She can no longer see him, can no longer recall his features or his silhouette, and has almost forgotten his eyes. And yet this image is all she has of him. She panics at the thought that she might lose this image, and that her desire – which admittedly tortures her, but which is now part and parcel of her, since she has entirely taken refuge in it, having fled from everything else, and to which she clings as one clings to one's own self-preservation, to life itself whether good or bad – might evaporate and that the only thing left would be a feeling of dreamlike malaise and suffering, of which she would no longer know the objective cause, would not even see him in her thoughts and would no longer be able to cherish him there. But all at once the image of M. de Laléande has returned, after that momentary disturbance in her inner vision. Her grief can resume its course – and this is almost an occasion for joy.

How will Mme de Breyves be able to tolerate going back to Paris, where he will not be returning until January? What will she do in the meantime? What will she do, what will he do afterwards?

Twenty times over I have been ready to leave for Biarritz and bring back M. de Laléande. The consequences might well be dreadful; but there is no point asking her, she will not permit it. But I am so saddened to see her delicate forehead being beaten from within and almost broken by the merciless blows of that inexplicable love. It gives her whole life an anguished rhythm. Often she imagines that he is about to arrive in Trouville, and will come up to her and tell her he loves her. She can see him: his eyes are shining. He talks to her with that expressionless, dreamlike voice that forbids us to believe while at the same time forcing us to listen. It is him. He is saying to her those words that make us delirious, even though we never hear them except in a dream, when we see shining in them, so heart-meltingly, the divine and trustful smile of destinies that are conjoined. Whereupon, the feeling that the two worlds, that of reality and that of her desire, run in parallel, and that it is just as impossible for them to meet as it is impossible for a shadow to coincide with the body that has cast it, awakens her. Then, remembering that minute near the cloakroom when his elbow brushed against hers, when he offered her that body which she could now be holding tight to hers if she had only wanted to, if she had only known, and which is now forever distant, she feels cries of despair and rebellion resounding through her entire body like those one hears on sinking ships. If, when out walking on the beach or in the woods, she allows herself gently to yield to the pleasure of contemplation or reverie, no, not even that – to a sweet smell, or a song brought to her indistinctly by the breeze, making her forget for a moment her pain, then she suddenly feels, striking deep into her heart, an agonising wound, and above the waves or the leaves, in the uncertain distance of the sylvan or marine horizon, she perceives the evanescent image of her invisible and ever-present victor who, his eyes shining through the clouds as on the day he offered himself to her, takes flight, bearing the quiver from which he has just sent yet one more arrow winging its way towards her.

– *July 1893*

PORTRAITS OF PAINTERS

ALBERT CUYP

Cuyp, a setting sun dissolved in limpid air –
A ripple of grey wood-pigeons, as if through water –
A damp golden haze, a halo for ox or birch,
Blue incense of fine days – smoke on the slopes –
Or gleam of stagnant marsh in the empty sky.
Cavaliers are ready, a pink plume in their hats;
Hands dangle down; the chill air makes their skin
Turn pink, and gently lifts their fine blond curls,
And, tempted by the hot fields and cool rills –
Their noise leaves undisturbed the herd of oxen
Dreaming in the mist of pale gold and repose –
They trot off, to breathe in those deep moments.

PAULUS POTTER

The mournful gloom of skies a uniform grey,
Made even sadder by rare patches of blue –
Filtering down onto the frozen plains
The warm tears of a foreign-seeming sun…
Potter, melancholy mood of sombre plains
That stretch out endlessly, joyless and dull,
The hamlet and the trees that shed no shade,
The scrubby gardens where no flower grows.
A ploughman drags his buckets home; his mare,
Sickly, resigned, disquieted, full of dreams
And anxious thoughts, lifting her thoughtful head,
Snuffles and sniffs and smells the whistling wind.

ANTOINE WATTEAU

The dusk applies make-up to trees and faces,
In its blue coat, beneath its dubious mask;
A scatter of kisses falls on weary lips...
The vague grows fond now, and the near grows far.

The masquerade is sad and distant too,
Love's movements now seem forced, with their sad charm.
A poet's whim – or lover's wise precaution,
Since love must be adorned with expert skill –
Behold: a ship, a picnic, silence, song.

ANTHONY VAN DYCK

Heart's gentle pride, and noble grace of things
That shine in eyes, in velvet, and in woods,
The lofty language of a posture's pose
– Hereditary pride of kings and ladies! –
You triumph, Van Dyck, prince of tranquil gestures,
In all the lovely things that will soon die,
In every lovely hand that can still open,
And unawares – who cares? – gives you the palm!
The horsemen halt, beneath the pines and near
The waves equally calm and near to tears –
Such royal children, grave already and splendid,
Resigned in dress, with brave-plumed hats and jewels
In which there weeps – as water through the flames –
The bitterness of tears that fill their souls
Too haughty to shed tears from open eyes;
And you, oh precious stroller, above all,
In pale blue shirt, one hand perched on your hip
(The other holds a fruit just plucked and leafy),
I dream, but do not grasp, your eyes and gestures:
Standing in alert repose in that dark shelter,

Oh wise young Richmond – charming madman too?
I come to you again: around your neck
A sapphire shines as quietly as your gaze.

PORTRAITS OF MUSICIANS

CHOPIN

Oh Chopin, sea of sighs and tears and sobs,
The butterflies wing their restless way across you,
Playing on sadness, or dancing on the waves.
You dream, love, suffer, cry, console, and charm
And cradle, and between each pain you bring
Dizzy and sweet oblivion at your whim
Like butterflies that dart from flower to flower;
Your joy is then in league with all your sorrow:
The torrid pain leaves us athirst for tears.
Oh pale and gentle friend of moon and waves,
Prince of despair or *grand seigneur* betrayed,
Your exultation grows, more palely beautiful,
As the sunlight floods into your sickroom, which
Weeps through its smiles and grieves to see the sun
Smile with regret and shed its tears for Hope!

GLUCK

Temple to love, to friendship, and to courage
Which a marquise erected in her English
Gardens, where many a Watteau cupid bends
Its bow and takes wild aim at noble hearts.

But the German artist – she would have dreamt of him
On Cnidus! – grave and deep sculpted the gods

And lovers, plain and bold, there on the frieze:
Hercules has his pyre in Armida's gardens!

The dancers' heels no longer kick the path
Where eyes now dust and smiles now blotted out
Muffle our steps and make the distance blue;
The harpsichord is cracked or silent now.

But your mute cry, Admetus, Iphigenia,
Still terrifies us, proffered by your body
And, vanquished by Orpheus, scorned by Alcestis too,
The Styx without masts or sky – where your genius anchored.

And Gluck like Alcestis has overcome by Love
The death that conquers every age's foibles;
He stands erect, august temple to courage
On the ruins of the little shrine to Love.

SCHUMANN

From the old friendly garden where you are made welcome,
You hear boys and nests whistling in the hedgerows,
Lovers weary of long journeys and wounds.
Schumann, wistful soldier, unsatisfied by war.

The cheerful breeze – a flock of doves goes by –
Fills the great walnut's shade with jasmine sweet,
The child reads the future from the flickering flames,
The cloud or wind speaks to your heart of tombs.

Once your tears flowed to the cries of the carnival
Or mingled gently with the bitter victory
Whose crazed momentum still shudders in your memory;
You may as well weep for good – *She* has betrayed you.

Towards Cologne the Rhine's sacred waters flow.
Ah, how gaily you sang on its banks, on holidays!
But now, broken and sorrowful, you sleep…
Tears rain down in the fitful gleam of darkness.

A dream (she lives, though dead, and the ingrate
Keeps faith); your hopes bloom fresh, his crime has crumbled
To dust… A lightning flash sears you awake:
Again its lash, as if for the first time…

Flow on, give balm, parading to the drums,
Be lovely… Schumann! Friend of souls and flowers,
Between the banks of joy, the waves of pain,
Oh holy river, garden fond, fresh, faithful,
Where moon and lilies kiss, and swallows too:
Army arrayed; dream, child; and, woman, weep.

MOZART

There's an Italian girl in the Bavarian prince's arms
(His sad and frozen eyes gleam at her softness!).
In his chilly gardens he holds tight to his heart
Her darkness-ripened breasts whose light he sucks.

His tender German soul – how deep its sigh! –
Enjoys at last the lazy pleasures of love,
And he grants to hands too weak to hold it fast
The radiant hope of his enchanted head.

Cherubino, Don Giovanni! Remember to forget
The flowers and sweet perfumes, all trampled, scattered
(But the tears flow on) from the gardens of Andalusia
To the tombs of Tuscany – blown by the winds!

In the German park where the mists gather like problems,
The Italian girl is still Queen of the Night.
Her breathing is a sweet and witty aria
And her Magic Flute lovingly tongues,
In the shadow still warm from the fine day's farewell,
The cool of sherbet, kisses and the sky.

THE CONFESSION OF A YOUNG WOMAN

The desires of the senses drag you hither and thither, but once their hour is past, what do you bring back? Remorse of conscience and dissipation of spirit. You set out in joy and you often return in sadness, and the pleasures of evening sadden the next morning. Thus the joys of the senses caress us at first, but in the end they wound and kill.
(*The Imitation of Christ*, I, 18)

1

Through the oblivion sought in drunken pleasures
There wafts, more sweet and virginal, heaven-sent,
The lilac with its melancholy scent.
(Henri de Régnier)

At last my deliverance is drawing near. I admit it: I was clumsy, I didn't shoot straight, I almost missed myself. Of course, it would have been better to die at the first shot, but in any case they weren't able to extract the bullet and then my heart started to behave erratically. It can't be long now. And yet – a week! It might last a whole week! And during that time I won't be able to do anything but strive to grasp the whole horrible chain of circumstances. If I were not so weak, if I had enough willpower to get out of bed and go away, I would like to die at Les Oublis, in the grounds where I spent all my summers until the age of fifteen. No place is more full of my mother, so much did her presence, and even more her absence, impregnate it with her whole person. Is not absence, for anyone who loves, the most certain, the most efficacious, the most vivacious, the most indestructible, and the most faithful of presences?

My mother would take me to Les Oublis at the end of April, leaving after two days, spending another two days there in the middle of May, then coming to fetch me in the last week in June. Her stays, so short, were the sweetest and yet cruellest things. During those two days she would lavish on me an affection of which she was usually very chary, as she was trying to make me tougher and to calm my unhealthy over-sensitivity. On the two evenings she spent at Les Oublis, she would come and say goodnight to me in my bed, an old habit she had otherwise given up, since it gave me too much pleasure and too much pain; I wouldn't be able to get to sleep since I kept calling her back to say goodnight to me all over again, eventually not daring to do so any more, but feeling all the more passionately my need for her, and constantly inventing new pretexts – my burning pillow that needed turning over, my frozen feet that she alone would be able to warm up in her hands… So many sweet moments were made even sweeter because I felt these were the moments at which my mother was really herself, and that her habitual frigidity must be something she imposed on herself with an effort. The day on which she set off again – a day of despair when I would cling to her skirts all the way to the train compartment, begging her to take me with her to Paris – I could clearly distinguish what was sincere from what was feigned: the sadness evident behind her cheerful, cross rebukes at my 'silly, ridiculous' sadness that she was trying to teach me to overcome, but which she shared. I can still feel the emotion I felt on one of those days of departure (that precise emotion, intact and unaffected by its painful return today), one of those days of departure when I made the welcome discovery of her tenderness, so similar and superior to mine. As with all discoveries, I had had an inkling of it before, but the facts seemed so often to tell against it! My sweetest impressions are those of the years when she returned to Les Oublis, having been summoned there because I was ill. Not only was she paying me an extra visit that I had not been expecting, but, above all, on those occasions she was nothing but the gentleness and tenderness that she lavished on me at length, without dissimulation or constraint. Even then, when that gentleness and tenderness had not been made even more gentle and tender by the thought that one day they would no longer be there for me, they counted for so much that the charm of convalescence always filled me with mortal sadness: the day approached on which I would again be well enough for my mother to leave, and until then I was not poorly enough for her to reassume the sternness and unyielding sense of justice that she had previously shown.

One day, the uncles with whom I lived at Les Oublis had kept concealed from me the fact that my mother was about to arrive, since a young cousin had come to spend a few hours with me, and I would not have paid him enough attention if I had been filled with the joyful anguish of that expectation. This little secret was perhaps the first of the circumstances independent of my will that helped to foster all the predispositions towards evil that, like all children of my age (and in those days no more than them) I bore within me. This young cousin who was fifteen – I was fourteen – was already extremely prone to vice and taught me things that immediately made me shudder with remorse and pleasure. In listening to him, in letting his hands stroke mine, I tasted a joy poisoned at its very source; soon I found the strength to leave him, and I ran off into the grounds filled with a mad desire for my mother whom I knew to be, alas! in Paris; I called out to her everywhere, in spite of myself, up and down the paths of the park. Suddenly, walking past an arbour, I spotted her on a bench, smiling and opening her arms for me. She lifted her veil to kiss me, I flung myself at her cheeks, bursting into tears; I wept for a long time, telling her all those nasty things that only the ignorance of my age could allow me to tell her and that she contrived to listen to with divine patience, without understanding them, but diminishing their importance with her kindness and thereby taking a load off my conscience. It grew lighter and lighter, this load; my crushed, humiliated soul rose, ever lighter and ever more powerful, overflowing so much that I was pure soul. A divine sweetness radiated from my mother and from my restored innocence. I immediately smelled under my nostrils an odour just as pure and just as fresh. It was a lilac tree, a branch of which, hidden by my mother's parasol, had already blossomed and was invisibly filling the air with its balm. High in the trees, the birds were singing with all their strength. Higher up, between the tree tops, the sky was of a blue so deep that it seemed but the entrance of a heaven into which it would be possible endlessly to rise. I kissed my mother. Never again did I experience the sweetness I then found in that kiss. She left the next day, and that departure was crueller than all those which had preceded it. As well as joy, it seemed to me as if the strength and the support that I needed, now that I had sinned for the first time, were abandoning me.

All these separations taught me in spite of myself that one day, the irreparable would happen, even though never at that time did I seriously envisage the possibility of surviving my mother. I was resolved to kill myself the minute she died. Later on, absence taught me even more bitter lessons: that one gets used to absence, and that the greatest diminishment of self, the most humiliating form of suffering, consists in realising that it no longer causes you any suffering. These lessons were in any case to be shown as false by subsequent events. Above all, right now, I am thinking back to the little garden where I would have my breakfast with my mother and where there were innumerable pansies. They had always seemed somewhat sad to me, as grave as emblems, but gentle and velvety, often mauve, sometimes violet, almost black, with gracious and mysterious yellow images, some of them entirely white and frail in their innocence. I pick them all now, in my memory, those pansies; their sadness has increased the more I have come to understand it, and the gentleness of their velvety down has disappeared for good.

2

How has all that freshwater surge of memories managed to spring up again and flow into my soul, today so impure, without being sullied by it? What virtue is possessed by that morning odour of lilacs that enables it to make its way across so many foetid vapours without being affected and weakened by them? Alas! the soul I had at fourteen can still awaken within me, but at the same time it is far away from me and outside of me. I know full well it is no longer my soul and that it is no longer within my power to make it so again. And yet at that time I did not think I would one day look back on it with nostalgia. It was merely pure, and I needed to make it strong, and capable of performing, one day, the highest tasks. Often, at Les Oublis, after going with my mother to the edge of the pond filled with the playful glitter of the sunlight and the fish, in the heat of the day, or in the morning and evening walking with her out in the fields, I would trustingly dream of the future that was never beautiful enough to satisfy her love, nor my desire to please her; and the powers, if not of will, at least of imagination and feeling that were stirring within me tumultuously summoned the destiny in which they could find fulfilment, and knocked repeatedly against the walls of my heart as if to burst through and rush out of me, into life. If I then jumped up, filled with exuberance; if I kissed my mother a thousand times over, ran far ahead like a puppy dog, or, having lingered behind her, picking poppies and cornflowers, brought them up to her with glad cries, it was less because of the joy of the walk itself and the pleasure of picking those flowers than it was a way of giving free rein to my happiness at sensing within me all the life ready to spring forth, to spread out infinitely, in vaster and more magical perspectives than those granted by the distant horizon of the forests and the sky that I wished I could reach at a single bound. Bouquets of cornflowers, clover and poppies, if I carried you off in such intoxication, my eyes burning, quivering all over – if you made me laugh and cry – the reason was that I made you part of all the hopes I then nursed, which now, like you, have withered and perished, and without having even blossomed like you, have returned to dust.

What made my mother so sad was my lack of will-power. I did everything on a momentary impulse. As long as my life drew its sustenance from my mind or my heart, it was, if not altogether good, at least not altogether bad. My mother and I were above all else preoccupied by the attempt to fulfil all my fine plans for work, tranquillity, and reasonableness, since we sensed – she more distinctly, I confusedly, but with great force – that this fulfilment would only come about if I could create by myself and within myself that will-power that she had conceived and nursed into existence. But each time, I would put it off to the next day. I let myself take my time; I was sometimes sorry to see time passing, but there was still so much of it ahead of me! And yet I was rather afraid, and felt vaguely that the habit of abstaining from exercising my will-power was starting to weigh on me more and more heavily, the more the years went by, filled as I was with the melancholy suspicion that things would not change all of a sudden, and that I could hardly count, if my life were to be transformed and my will-power shaped, on some miracle that would cost me no effort at all. To desire strength of will was not enough. I would have needed to do just what I could not do without strength of will: will it.

And the crazed wind of concupiscence
Makes your flesh crack and flap like an old flag.
(Baudelaire)

In the course of my sixteenth year, I suffered a breakdown that left me feeling ill. To take my mind off it, my parents decided to bring me out into society. Young men fell into the habit of coming to see me. One of them was perverse and spiteful. He had manners that were both gentle and over-bold. He was the one I fell in love with. My parents learnt of it, and didn't do anything too hasty, in case they upset me too much. Spending all the time I couldn't see him thinking about him, I finally lowered myself to resemble him as much as I possibly could. He led me into evil ways almost by stealth, then got me into the habit of allowing bad thoughts arise in me, thoughts which I had no strength of will to oppose – and will alone would have been the only power capable of forcing them back into the infernal shadow from which they had emerged. When my love for him faded, habit had taken its place, and there was no lack of immoral young men ready to exploit it. They were partners in my crimes, and made themselves the apologists of my misdeeds before the tribunal of my conscience. At first I was filled with agonised remorse, I made confessions that were not understood. My comrades put me off the idea of persisting in trying to tell my father. They slowly persuaded me that all girls did the same and that parents merely pretended not to know. My imagination soon glossed over the lies that I was ceaselessly obliged to tell by keeping a silence that my imagination depicted as the necessary result of some ineluctable necessity. At this time I was no longer properly living; but I was still dreaming, thinking and feeling.

To take my mind off all these unwholesome desires and chase them away, I started to go out a great deal into society. Its desiccating pleasures accustomed me to living in company the whole time, and as I lost the taste for solitude, I lost the secret of the joys that nature and art had hitherto given me. Never did I go to concerts so frequently as I did in those years. Never, entirely preoccupied as I was with the desire of being admired as I sat in some elegant box, did I have less of a feeling for the music. I listened, but I heard nothing. If by chance I *did* hear, I had ceased to see everything that music can reveal. My walks too had been, as it were, stricken with sterility. The things which had once sufficed to make me happy for a whole day – a ray of sunlight casting its yellow beams on the grass, the odour given off by damp leaves when the last drops of rain fell – had, like me, lost their sweetness and gaiety. The woods, the sky, the lakes and rivers seemed to turn away from me, and if, lingering alone with them face to face, I anxiously questioned them, they no longer murmured those vague replies that had once so ravished me. The divine guests that are announced by the voice of the waters, leaves and sky only ever deign to visit hearts which, by dwelling within themselves, have purified themselves.

It was at this point that, seeking an inverse remedy, and not being courageous enough to will the true remedy that lay so close to me, and, alas! so far away from me, since it was within me, I again let myself go, succumbing to guilty pleasures, thinking thereby to revive the flame which society had extinguished. It was in vain. Held back by the pleasure I took in pleasing others, I kept putting off, day after day, the definitive decision, the choice, the really free act – namely, opting for solitude. I did not give up one of these two vices for the other. I combined them. More than that: each vice assumed the responsibility of overcoming all the obstacles in thought and feeling that might have stood in the way of the other vice, and thus seemed actually to summon it into being. I would go out into society to calm myself after some misdemeanour, and I would commit another one the minute I was calm. It was at that terrible period, after the loss of innocence, and before the remorse I feel today, at that period when, of all the periods in my life, I was most worthless, that I was most highly esteemed by everyone else. I had been considered as a pretentious and eccentric little girl; now, conversely, the ashes of my imagination were greatly to the taste of society, which delighted in them. Just when I was committing the greatest of crimes against my mother, I was viewed, because of my tenderly respectful manner towards her, as a model daughter. After the suicide of my mind, everyone admired my intelligence and doted on my spirited remarks. My desiccated imagination, my choked sensibility, were enough to quench the thirst of those who most craved spiritual life, so artificial was their thirst, and so mendacious – just like the source at which they all imagined they could slake it! In any case, no one suspected the secret crime of my life, and I seemed to everyone to be the ideal young girl. How many parents told my mother at that time that if I had not enjoyed such a high position and if they had been able to aspire to me, they would have wished for no other wife for their sons! In the depths of my obliterated conscience, I nonetheless felt at this undeserved praise a desperate sense of shame; this shame did not reach the surface, and I had fallen so low that I was vile enough to report their praise, sarcastically, to my partners in crime.

4

I think of all who have lost what can
Never, ever be found again!
(Baudelaire)

In the winter of my twentieth year, my mother's health, which had never been strong, was greatly impaired. I learnt that she had a heart disease, not a grave one, but one that still meant she needed to avoid any upset. One of my uncles told me that my mother wished to see me married. A specific and important duty presented itself to me. I would be able to prove to my mother how much I loved her. I accepted the first marriage request that she passed on to me, and, by agreeing to it, I charged necessity with the task which will-power had been unable to make me undertake: that of changing my life. My fiancé was exactly the man who, with his exceptional intelligence, his gentleness and his vigour, could have the most salutary influence on me. He was, in addition, resolved to live with us. I would no longer be separated from my mother, which would have been the cruellest of pains for me.

Then I plucked up the courage to tell my confessor of all my misdeeds. I asked him if I should admit them to my fiancé too. He was compassionate enough to dissuade me, but made me swear that I would never relapse into those errors, and gave me absolution. The belated flowers that joy made blossom in my heart – a heart that I had thought was forever sterile – bore fruit. The grace of God, the grace of youth – in which we see so many wounds closing of themselves, thanks to the vitality of that time of life – had cured me. If, as St Augustine says, it is more difficult to become chaste once one has lost the habit of chastity, then I really experienced how difficult virtue can be. No one suspected that I was an immeasurably better person now than I had been previously, and every day my mother would kiss my brow which she had never ceased to think of as pure without knowing that it was now regenerate. Indeed, I was at this period unjustly rebuked for my inattentiveness, my silence and my melancholy in society. But these rebukes did not annoy me: the secret that I shared with my satisfied conscience gave me a pleasure altogether sufficient. The convalescence of my soul – which now ceaselessly smiled on me with a face like that of my mother, and gazed at me with an expression of tender reproach through its drying tears – was imbued with boundless charm and languor. Yes, my soul was experiencing a rebirth. I myself could not understand how I had been able to mistreat it, make it suffer, almost kill it. And I effusively thanked God for having saved it in time.

It was the harmony between this pure and profound joy on the one hand, and the fresh serenity of the sky on the other, that I was busy enjoying on the evening when *it all finally happened*. The absence of my fiancé, who had gone to spend a couple of days with his sister, the presence at dinner of the young man who bore the greatest share of responsibility for my former errors, did not cast the slightest sadness over that limpid May evening. There was not a cloud in the sky, which in all its perfect clarity was reflected in my heart. In addition, my mother, as if there had been a mysterious solidarity between her and my soul – despite her total ignorance of my misdeeds – was more or less fully cured. 'She needs lots of tender loving care from you over the next fortnight,' the doctor had said, 'and after that, she's in no risk of a relapse!' These words alone were for me the promise of a future of happiness whose sweetness made me burst into tears. That evening, my mother was wearing a more elegant dress than usual, and, for the first time since my father's death, even though that was now a good ten years ago, she had added a dash of mauve to her habitual black dress. She was quite abashed to have dressed like this, in the clothes she had worn when she was younger, and both sad and happy to have forced herself to do violence to her grief and mourning so as to give me pleasure and celebrate my joy. I held up to her bodice a pink carnation which at first she brushed away, but then pinned to her clothing – since it came from me – albeit with a rather hesitant and embarrassed hand. Just as we were about to sit down at table, I pulled her face towards me, as we stood near the window – her face now fresh and rejuvenated after her past sufferings – and I passionately kissed her. I had been wrong to say that I had never again experienced the sweetness of our kiss at Les Oublis. The kiss I gave her on that evening was as sweet as any other. Or rather, it was the very same kiss as that at Les Oublis which, summoned by the attractive force of a similar moment, wafted gently up from the depths of the past and came to place itself between my mother's still somewhat pallid cheeks and my lips.

A toast was raised to my forthcoming marriage. I only ever drank water because of the over-excitement that wine aroused in my nerves. My uncle declared that, at a moment like this, I could make an exception. I can see in front of my eyes his cheerful face as he uttered those stupid words… My God! My God! I have confessed everything so calmly, am I going to be obliged to stop here? I can no longer see straight! Oh yes… my uncle said that I could, after all, make an exception at a moment like this. He looked at me laughingly as he said these words; I drank quickly, before glancing at my mother, in case she forbade me. She said gently, 'One should never yield an inch to evil, however insignificant it seems'. But the champagne was so cool that I drank another two glasses. My head had become really heavy; I needed simultaneously to rest and to discharge my nervous tension. Everyone was getting up from table; Jacques came over to me and said, as he stared at me:

'Come with me, please; I'd like to show you some poetry I've written.'

His handsome eyes twinkled above his fresh young cheeks, and he was slowly twirling his moustache. I realised I was destroying myself and I had no strength to resist. Trembling all over, I said:

'Yes, I'd love to.'

It was in uttering these words, or even earlier, in drinking the second glass of champagne, that I committed the really deliberate act, the abominable act. After that, I merely let myself go. We had locked both doors, and he, his breath on my cheeks, held me tight, his hands wandering feverishly up and down my body. Then, as pleasure started to overwhelm me, I felt arising in the depths of my heart a boundless desolation and sadness; it seemed that I was making them all weep – the soul of my mother, the soul of my guardian angel, the soul of God. I had never been able to read without a shudder of horror the account of the torture that evildoers inflict on animals, on their own wives, on their children; it appeared to me now, indistinctly, that in every pleasurable and sinful action the body in thrall to rapture is just as fierce as they are; within us, just as many good intentions, and just as many pure angels weep as they suffer martyrdom.

Soon my uncles would have finished their game of cards and would be coming back. We would do it before they returned, I would never again yield, this was the last time… Then, above the fireplace, I saw myself in the mirror. None of the diffuse anguish of my soul was painted on my face, but from my shining eyes to my burning cheeks and my proffered lips, everything in that face breathed a sensual, stupid and brutal joy. Then I thought of the horror anyone would feel who had seen me just now kissing my mother with melancholy tenderness, and could now see me thus transformed into a beast. But immediately there arose in the mirror, against my face, Jacques's mouth, avid beneath his moustache. Shaken to my depths, I moved my head towards his, when opposite me I saw – yes, I am telling it to you just as it happened, listen to me since I can tell you – on the balcony, outside the window, I saw my mother gazing at me, horror-struck. I don't know if she cried out, I heard nothing, but she fell backwards and remained with her head caught between the two bars of the railing…

This isn't the last time I'll be telling you my story: as I said, I almost missed myself; even though I'd taken careful aim, I did not shoot straight. But they were not able to extract the bullet and my heart has started to behave erratically. But I can linger on for a week in this state, and until then I'll be constantly trying to understand how it all started, and *seeing* how it finished. I would have preferred my mother to see me commit yet other crimes – or even that particular one, but without her catching sight of the expression of joy that my face had in the mirror. No, she can't possibly have seen it... It was a coincidence... She was struck down by apoplexy a minute before she saw me... She didn't see that expression... It's not possible! God, who knew everything, would never have allowed it.

A DINNER IN TOWN

*But, Fundanius, who shared with you
the pleasures of that meal? I am longing
to know.*
(Horace)

1

Honoré was late; he said hello to the hosts, to the guests he knew, was introduced to the others, and went to sit down at table. After a few moments, his neighbour, a very young man, asked him to name the guests and tell him something about them. Honoré had never met him in society until now. He was very handsome. The hostess kept gazing at him with burning eyes that indicated quite well enough why she had invited him, and showed that he would soon be part of her circle. Honoré sensed within him the potential for future greatness, but, without any envy, out of polite benevolence, he decided it was his duty to reply. He looked around. Opposite, two neighbours were not talking to each other; they had been invited together, out of clumsy good intentions, and placed next to each other because they were both active in literature. But on top of this initial reason for hating each other, they had a more specific one. The older, a kinsman – doubly hypnotised – of M. Paul Desjardins and M. de Vogüé, affected a scornful silence towards the younger man, the favourite disciple of M. Maurice Barrès, who considered him in turn with a certain irony. Furthermore, the ill will each of them felt exaggerated – greatly against their respective desires – the importance of the other, as if the chief of rogues had been forced to confront the king of imbeciles. Further along, a superb Spanish woman was eating in a furious temper. She had unhesitatingly – being a serious kind of person – sacrificed a lovers' tryst this evening to the probability that she might advance her social career by coming to dinner in an elegant household. And indeed, there was every likelihood that she had made the right choice. The snobbery of Mme Fremer was for her lady friends, and the snobbery of her lady friends was for Mme Fremer, like a mutual insurance against becoming commonplace and bourgeois. But chance had so willed it that Mme Fremer was selling off, on just this very evening, a stock of people she hadn't had time to invite to her dinners before – people to whom, for different reasons, she really wanted to be polite, and whom she had assembled almost at random. The whole gathering was suitably crowned by a duchess, but one whom the Spanish woman already knew and who was of no further interest to her. And so she kept exchanging angry glances with her husband, whose guttural voice could always be heard at these evening receptions saying successively (leaving between each request an interval of five minutes suitably filled with other little tasks), 'Would you please introduce me to the Duke?' And, to the Duke, 'Monsieur, would you please introduce me to the Duchess?' And, to the Duchess, 'Madame, may I introduce my wife to you?' Exasperating at having to waste his time, he had nonetheless resigned himself to striking up a conversation with his neighbour, the associate of the master of the house. For over a year, Fremer had been begging his wife to invite this man. She had finally yielded and had hidden him away between the Spanish woman's husband and a humanist. The humanist, an omnivorous reader, was also an omnivorous eater. Quotations and burps kept welling from his lips, and these two disagreeable characteristics were equally repugnant to the woman next to him, a noble commoner, Mme Lenoir. She had soon brought the conversation round to the victories of the Prince des Buivres in Dahomey and said in a voice tremulous with emotion, 'Dear boy, how delighted I am to see him honouring his family!' She was indeed a cousin of the Buivres, who, all being younger than she was, treated her with the deference due to her age, her attachment to the royal family, her huge fortune and the unfailing sterility of her three marriages. She had transferred to the entire Buivres clan all the family feelings of which she was capable. She took personal umbrage when any of them so misbehaved that he had to be put under legal guardianship; and, around her right-thinking brow, on the parting in her Orleanist hair, she naturally wore the laurels of the family member who happened to be a General. Initially an intruder into that hitherto so exclusive family, she had become its head and, as it were, its dowager. She felt really exiled in modern society, and always spoke with nostalgic affection of the 'gentlemen of bygone days'. Her snobbery was all in her imagination: indeed, her imagination contained nothing else. Names rich in history and glory exerted a singular influence on her sensitive mind, and she took great delight, quite devoid of self-interest, in dining with princes or reading memoirs from the Ancien Régime. She always wore the same raisin-bedecked hats, which were as invariable as her principles. Her eyes sparkled with inanity. Her smiling face was noble, her affected gestures exaggerated and meaningless. Thanks to her trust in God, she was in a similarly optimistic flutter on the eve of a garden party or a revolution, and made darting little gestures that seemed designed to ward off radicalism or bad weather. Her neighbour the humanist was talking to her with wearisome eloquence and a dreadfully facile gift for the right formula; he kept quoting Horace to excuse his gluttony and drunkenness in the eyes of others, and to add a poetic sheen to those failings in his own. Invisible, ancient and yet freshly-plucked roses wreathed his narrow brow. But with an equal politeness, which came to her easily since she found in it a way of exerting her influence and showing her respect – nowadays rare – for old traditions, Mme Lenoir turned every five minutes or so to talk to M. Fremer's associate. The latter had, in any case, no cause for complaint. From the other end of the table, Mme Fremer was addressing to him the most charming flatteries. She wanted this dinner to count for several years' worth and, resolved not to have to invite this wet blanket for a long time to come, she was burying him under garlands of praise. As for M. Fremer, who worked all day at his bank and then in the evening found himself being dragged out into society by his wife, or forced to stay at home if they were giving a reception, he was always ready to eat anyone alive, but always muzzled, so that he had ended up by putting on, in the most everyday circumstances, an expression compounded of muted irritation, sulky resignation, barely contained exasperation, and profound brutishness. However, on this particular evening, this expression on the financier's face had given way to a cordial satisfaction every time that his eyes met those of his associate. Although he couldn't stand him in the ordinary course of things, he had discovered in himself feelings of fleeting but sincere affection for him, not because he found it easy to dazzle him with his opulence, but because of that same vague fellow-feeling that overcomes us when we are abroad and see a Frenchman, even an odious one. He, so violently torn away every evening from his habits, so unjustly deprived of the rest he had deserved, so cruelly uprooted, at last felt a bond, one that usually filled him with violent resentment, but strong nonetheless, which made him feel close to someone and meant that he could emerge and even escape from his fierce and desperate isolation. Opposite him, Mme Fremer allowed the enchanted eyes of her fellow diners to reflect her blonde beauty. The double reputation which surrounded her like an aura was a deceiving prism through which everyone tried to distinguish her true features. An ambitious woman, an intriguer, almost an adventurer – or so it was said in the world of finance that she had abandoned for a more brilliant destiny – she appeared, on the contrary, in the eyes of the *faubourg* and the royal family (whom she had quite won over with her superior intelligence), an angel of gentleness and virtue. In addition, she had not forgotten her old and humbler friends, and remembered them in particular when they were ill or bereaved – those touching circumstances which had the added advantage that, since they then of course stayed at home instead of going out into society, they could not complain about not being invited anywhere. Hence she gave full rein to her charitable impulses, and in her conversations with relatives or priests at the bedside of the dying, she shed sincere tears, killing little by little the remorse that her excessively easy life inspired in her scrupulous heart.

But the most likeable guest was the young Duchess of D***, whose clear, alert mind, never anxious or confused, contrasted so strangely with the incurable melancholy of her lovely eyes, the pessimism of her lips, the boundless and noble weariness of her hands. This energetic lover of life in every shape and form – kindness, literature, theatre, action, and friendship – kept biting, without spoiling them, like a flower cast aside, her beautiful red lips, whose corners a disenchanted smile barely raised. Her eyes seemed to indicate a mind that had foundered once and for all on the sickly waters of regret. How many times, in the street, at the theatre, had wistful passers-by allowed those variable stars to illuminate their dreams! Just now the Duchess, who was busy remembering a vaudeville show, or inventing a new outfit, continued nonetheless to stretch out the joints of her noble fingers, looking resigned and pensive, and gazing around her with a deep and desperate expression in her eyes, drowning the impressionable guests in the torrents of their melancholy. Her exquisite conversation negligently decked itself out in the faded and perfectly charming elegance of an already old-fashioned scepticism. There had just been a heated discussion, and this woman, so absolute in life, convinced that there was only one way of dressing, would repeat to all and sundry, 'But why can't one say and think everything? I might be right, and so might you. How dreadful and narrow-minded it is to have an opinion.' Her mind was not like her body, dressed in the latest fashion, and she found it easy to tease symbolists and enthusiasts. But her mind rather resembled those charming women who are beautiful and vivacious enough to look good even when they are wearing old clothes. In any case, it was perhaps a deliberate coquetry. Certain excessively crude opinions would have paralysed her mind in the same way that, she was convinced, certain colours would have clashed with her complexion.

To his handsome neighbour, Honoré had given a rapid sketch of these different figures, and one which was so good-natured that, despite the profound differences between them, they all seemed alike – the brilliant Mme de Torreno, the witty Duchess of D***, the beautiful Mme Lenoir. He had neglected the only feature they all shared, or rather the same collective madness, the same prevalent epidemic by which they were all affected: snobbery. True, this snobbery assumed very different shapes in accordance with their very different natures, and there was a world of difference between the imaginative and poetic snobbery of Mme Lenoir and the all-conquering snobbery of Mme de Torreno, who was as avid as a civil servant desperate to reach the highest positions. And yet, that terrible woman was quite capable of rehumanising herself. Her neighbour had just told her that he had been admiring her daughter in the Parc Monceau. Immediately she had broken her angry silence. She had felt for this obscure accountant a pure and friendly gratitude that she would have been incapable of feeling for a prince, and now they were chatting away like old friends.

Mme Fremer was presiding over the conversations with the visible satisfaction that sprang from the sentiment of the lofty mission she was performing. Used to introducing great writers to duchesses, she seemed, in her own eyes, a sort of omnipotent Minister of Foreign Affairs who even in matters of protocol displayed great elevation of mind. In the same way, a spectator digesting his dinner in the theatre can see below him, as he sits in judgement over them, artists, audience, the rules of dramatic art, and genius. The conversation was in any case going with a real swing. They had reached that moment at dinner when gentlemen start touching the knees of the ladies next to them, or questioning them about their literary preferences: it depended on their different temperaments and education, and above all it depended on the ladies in question. One minute, a faux pas seemed inevitable. Honoré's handsome neighbour had tried with all the imprudence of youth to insinuate that in the work of Heredia there were perhaps more ideas than people were prepared to admit. The guests, seeing their habitual opinions being thrown into question, started to look morose. But Mme Fremer immediately exclaimed, 'On the contrary, they are merely admirable cameos, sumptuous enamels, flawless pieces of jewellery,' whereupon vivacity and satisfaction reappeared on every face. A discussion of the anarchists was a more serious matter. But Mme Fremer, as if bowing resignedly before some fateful and natural law, said slowly, 'What's the use of all that? Rich and poor will be always with us.' And all those people, the poorest of whom had an income of at least a hundred thousand pounds, struck by the truth of this remark, and freed from their scruples, emptied with buoyant gaiety their last glass of champagne.

2

After dinner

Honoré, aware that the mixture of different wines had left him feeling giddy, went off without saying goodbye, picked up his overcoat downstairs and started to walk down the Champs-Élysées. He was filled with great joy. The barriers of impossibility which separate our desires and our dreams from the realm of reality had been broken down, and his thoughts, filled with exaltation at their own momentum, circulated exuberantly through the domain of the unattainable.

The mysterious avenues that extend between one human being and another, and at the far end of which, every evening, there perhaps sets some unsuspected sun of joy or desolation, were starting to draw him down them. Each person he thought of immediately struck him as irresistibly likeable, and he turned successively down each street in which he might hope to meet them in turn; and if his expectations had been realised, he would have gone up and greeted strangers or indifferent passers-by fearlessly, gently, and with a quiver of anticipation. Now that a stage-set positioned too close to him had fallen away, life stretched out into the distance ahead of him, in all the charm of its novelty and its mystery, in friendly landscapes that beckoned him on. And the regret that it might be the mirage or the reality of a single evening filled him with despair; he would make sure he always dined and drank as well as he just had, so that he could again see things as lovely as these. He was simply pained at his inability to reach all the scenes dotted here and there in the infinite prospect that stretched away into the far distance. Then he was struck by the sound of his voice, somewhat rough and forced, that had been repeating for a quarter of an hour, 'Life is sad, how stupid!' (This last word was underlined by the abrupt gesture he made with his right arm, and he noticed the sudden jerk of his walking stick.) He told himself sadly that these mechanical words were an altogether banal translation of similar visions which, he thought, were perhaps not amenable to expression.

'Alas! No doubt the intensity of my pleasure or my regret is multiplied a hundredfold, but even so, its intellectual content remains the same. My happiness is edgy, personal, untranslatable to anyone else, and if I were to write now, my style would have the same qualities, the same defects, alas! and the same commonplace tenor as usual.' But the physical well-being he was feeling prevented him from thinking about it at any greater length and immediately gave him that supreme consolation, oblivion. He had come out onto the boulevards. People were going by, to whom he extended his warm feelings, certain that they would be reciprocated. He felt that he was their glorious role model; he opened his overcoat so that they could see the dazzling whiteness of his evening jacket, which so suited him, and the dark red carnation in his buttonhole. Thus he offered himself to the admiration of the passers-by and the affection which he so voluptuously exchanged with them.

NOSTALGIA – DAYDREAMS
UNDER CHANGING SKIES

> *So the poet's habit of living should be set on
> a key so low that the common influences
> should delight him. His cheerfulness should
> be the gift of the sunlight; the air should
> suffice for his inspiration, and he should be
> tipsy with water.*
> (Emerson)

1

Tuileries

In the garden of the Tuileries, this morning, the sun has dozed on
all the stone steps in turn, like a blond teenager whose slumber is
immediately interrupted by a passing cloud. Against the old palace, the
young shoots are a vivid green. The breath of the enchanted wind stirs
into the perfume of the past the fresh odour of lilacs. The statues, which
in our public squares are as alarming as hysterical women, here dream
away in their arbours like wise men under the glowing verdure which
protects their whiteness. The ponds in whose depths the blue sky lolls
at ease gleam like shining eyes. From the terrace at the water's edge one
can see, emerging from the old quai d'Orsay district, on the other side
of the river and as if in another century, a passing hussar. Bindweed
overflows in rank disorder from the pots crowned with geraniums.
Yearning for sunshine, the heliotrope burns its perfumes. Outside the
Louvre spring up groups of hollyhocks, as weightless as masts, as noble
and graceful as pillars, blushing like young girls. Iridescent in the
sunlight and sighing with love, the jets of water mount skywards. At the
end of the Terrace, a stone horseman, launched on a headlong but
immobile gallop, his lips glued to a joyous trumpet, incarnates all the
ardour of spring.

But the sky has clouded over; it's going to rain. The ponds, in which
the azure sky has ceased to shine, seem eyes empty of life or vessels

filled with tears. The absurd jet of water, whipped by the breeze, raises faster and faster skywards its now derisory hymn. The futile sweetness of the lilacs is infinitely sad. And over there, dashing headlong, his marble feet rousing with a furious and immobile movement the dizzying and static gallop of his horse, the unconscious horseman endlessly blows his trumpet against the black sky.

2

Versailles

> *A canal which makes the most eloquent conversationalists dreamy as soon as they draw near it, and where I always feel happy, whether my mood is sad or joyful.*
> (Letter from Balzac to M. de Lamothe-Aigron)

The exhausted autumn, no longer even warmed by the fleeting sun, loses one by one its last colours. The extreme ardour of its foliage, so filled with flame that the whole afternoon and even the morning created the glorious illusion of sunset, has completely faded. Only the dahlias, the French marigolds and the yellow, purple, white and pink chrysanthemums are still shining on autumn's dark and desolate face. At six o'clock in the evening, when you walk through the Tuileries uniformly grey and bare under the equally sombre sky, where the black trees describe branch by branch their powerful and subtle despair, you suddenly catch sight of a clump of autumn flowers that gleams richly in the darkness and does voluptuous violence to your eyes, used as they are to those ashen horizons. The morning hours are more mellow. The sun still shines, occasionally, and I can still see as I leave the terrace at the water's edge, along the great flights of stone steps, my shadow walking down the steps, one by one, in front of me. I would prefer not to evoke you here, after so many others have done so,* Versailles, great

* And particularly after MM. Maurice Barrès, Henri de Régnier, and Robert de Montesquiou-Fezensac.

sweet and rust-coloured name, royal cemetery of leaves and branches, vast waters and marble statues, a truly aristocratic and disheartening place, where we are not even troubled by remorse at the fact that the lives of so many workers here served only to refine and enlarge less the joys of another time than the melancholy of our own. I would prefer not to utter your name after so many others, and yet, how many times, from the red-hued basin of your pink marble ponds, have I drunk to the dregs, to the point of madness, the intoxicating and bitter sweetness of those last and loveliest autumn days. The earth mingled with withered leaves and rotten leaves seemed from afar a yellow and purple mosaic that had lost its gleam. Walking by the Hameau, lifting the colour of my overcoat against the wind, I could hear the cooing of doves. Everywhere the odour of boxwood, as on Palm Sunday, intoxicated me. How was it that I was still able to pick one more slender spring bouquet, in gardens ravaged by the autumn? On the water, the wind blew roughly on the petals of a shivering rose. In the great unleaving in the Trianon, only the delicate vault of a little bridge of white geranium lifted above the icy water its flowers barely bent by the breeze. To be sure, ever since I have breathed the wind coming in from the sea and the tang of salt in the sunken roads of Normandy, ever since I have seen the waves glittering through the branches of blossoming rhododendrons, I have known how much the vegetable world is made more graceful by the proximity of water. But how much more virginal was the purity of that gentle white geranium, leaning with graceful restraint over the wind-ruffled waters between their quays of dead branches! Oh silvery gleam of old age in the woods still green, oh weeping branches, ponds and lakes that a pious hand has placed here and there, like urns offered to the melancholy of the trees!

3

A walk

Despite the sky so pure and the sun already warm, the wind was still blowing just as cold and the trees were still as bare as in winter. To build a fire, I had to cut down one of those branches that I thought were dead, and the sap spurted from it, spattering my arm to the shoulder and betraying a tumultuous heart beneath the tree's icy bark. Between the trunks, the bare wintry ground was strewn with anemones, cowslips and violets, and the rivers, which even yesterday were dark and empty, were filled with a tender, blue and living sky lolling in their depths. Not that pale and wearied sky of the fine October evenings which, stretching out in the water's depths, seems to be dying of love and melancholy, but an intense and ardent sky on whose tender and cheerful azure sheen there passed at every moment, grey, blue and pink, not the shadows of the pensive clouds, but the glittering and gliding fins of a perch, an eel or a smelt. Drunk with joy, they darted between the sky and the weeds, in their meadows and under their forests that had, like ours, been filled with dazzling enchantment by the resplendent genie of spring. And flowing freshly over their heads, through their gills, beneath their bellies, the waters also rushed along, singing, and chasing merry sunbeams before them.

The farmyard where you had to go for eggs was no less attractive a sight. The sun, like an inspired and prolific poet who does not disdain to shed beauty over the humblest places that had seemed hitherto to fall outside the remit of art, was still warming the beneficent energies of the manure heap, the uneven cobbles of the yard, and the pear tree, its back bent like an old servant woman.

But who is this personage adorned in royal vestment advancing towards us, through this rustic farmyard scene, on the tip of its toes, as if to avoid getting dirty? It is the bird of Juno, gleaming not with lifeless jewels but with the very eyes of Argus – the peacock, whose fabulous luxury here takes us by surprise. Arrayed as on some feast day, a few moments before the arrival of the first guests, in her robe with its multicoloured train, an azure gorget already tied round her royal throat, and her head adorned with sprays, the hostess, a radiant figure, crosses her courtyard before the marvelling eyes of the curious onlookers gathered outside the railings, to go and give one final order or await a prince of the blood whom she is to receive on the very threshold.

No: it is here that the peacock spends its life, a veritable bird of paradise in a farmyard, between the turkeys and the hens, like captive Andromache spinning wool among the slaves, but unlike her not forced to shed the magnificence of the royal insignia and the hereditary jewels, an Apollo easy to recognise, even when he guards, still radiant, the herds of Admetus.

4

A family listening to music

> *For music is so sweet,*
> *It fills the soul, and like a choir, with heavenly art*
> *Awakes a thousand voices that sing within the heart.*[10]

For a family that is really alive, one in which every member thinks, loves and acts, a garden is a really welcome possession. On spring, summer and autumn evenings, everyone, now that their day's task is ended, gathers there; and however small the garden, however close its hedges, they are not so high that they prevent you from seeing a great expanse of sky to which everyone can raise his eyes, without speaking, as he dreams. The child dreams of his future plans, of the house where he will live with his favourite playmate from whom he need never again be separated, and of the mysteries of the earth and of life; the young man dreams of the mysterious charm of the woman he loves; the young woman dreams of her child's future; the wife who was once troubled at soul discovers, in these deep and lucid hours, that beneath her husband's cold exterior is hidden a painful regret, which fills her with pity. The father, following with his gaze the smoke rising over the roof, dwells on the peaceful scenes of his past which the evening light illuminates with a distant magical glow; he thinks of his imminent death, and the life his children will lead after his death; and thus the soul of the entire family ascends with religious feeling towards the setting sun, while the great lime, chestnut or pine tree casts over them all the blessing of its exquisite odour or its venerable shade.

But for a family that is really alive, one in which every member thinks, loves and acts, for a family which has a soul, how much sweeter it is, when evening comes, for this soul to be able to find embodiment in a voice, in the clear and inexhaustible voice of a young girl or a young man lucky enough to possess a gift for music and song. The stranger walking past the garden gate when the family is sitting in silence would fear, if he approached, to disturb the almost religious dream that each of them harbours; but if this stranger, without being able to hear the song, could see the gathering of friends and family listening, how much more he would imagine they were attending some invisible mass; in other words, despite their diverse postures, how much the resemblance between the expressions on their faces would demonstrate the true unity of their souls, attained for a few moments by the attraction they feel for one and the same ideal drama, by their communion with one and the same dream. Every now and then, just as the wind bends the grass and makes the branches sway to and fro, an unseen breath bends their heads or makes them look up suddenly. Then, as if a messenger invisible to you were recounting some exciting tale, all of them seem to be anxiously awaiting, listening with delight or terror to the same news which nonetheless arouses different echoes in each of them. The anguish of the music reaches a peak; its moments of aspiration suddenly collapse, only to be followed by even more desperate aspirations. Its boundless glowing expanses, its mysterious darkness, represent for the old man the vast spectacle of life and death, for the child the urgent promises of land and sea, for the man in love the mysterious infinity and the glowing darkness of passion. The thinker sees his inner life flow by in its entirety; the dying falls of the melody are his own dying falls, and his whole heart lifts and leaps forward again when the melody resumes its flight. The powerful murmur of the harmonies makes the rich dark depths of his memory quiver. The man of action starts breathing heavily at the clash of the chords, and the gallop of the *vivaces*; he triumphs majestically in the *adagios*. Even the unfaithful wife senses that the error of her ways has been pardoned, infinitised – an error which also took its divine origin from the dissatisfaction of a heart that had not been assuaged by the usual joys and had gone astray, but only because of its quest for mystery; its vastest aspirations are fulfilled by this music, full to the brim like the voice of church bells. The musician, despite claiming to enjoy in music only its technical side, also feels these meaningful emotions, but they are enveloped in his sense of musical beauty, a feeling which conceals those emotions from him. And last but not least, I myself, listening in music to the most vast and universal beauty of life and death, sea and sky, I also feel in it everything that is most individual and unique in your allure, my dearest beloved.

5

The paradoxes of today are the prejudices of tomorrow, since the coarsest and most unpleasant prejudices of today had their moment of novelty, in which fashion lent them its fragile grace. Many of today's women want to free themselves from all prejudices, and by 'prejudices' they mean 'principles'. That is *their* prejudice – a burdensome one, even though they adorn themselves with it as though it were a delicate and somewhat strange flower. They think that nothing has any hidden background; they put everything on the same level. They enjoy a book, or life itself, as if it were a nice day or an orange. They speak of the 'art' of a dressmaker or the 'philosophy' of 'Parisian life'. They would be abashed if they had to classify anything or judge anything, and say: this is good, this is bad. In former times, when a woman behaved well, it was as it were an act of vengeance on the part of her moral being – her thought – over her instinctual nature. Today, when a woman behaves well, it is an act of vengeance on the part of her instinctual nature over her moral being, i.e. her theoretical immorality (see the plays of MM. Halévy and Meilhac)[11]. Now that all moral and social bonds are growing really slack, women drift from this theoretical immorality to that instinctual goodness. They seek only pleasure and find it only when they are not seeking it, when they suffer involuntarily. This scepticism and this dilettantism would be shocking in books, like an old-fashioned piece of jewellery. But women, far from being the oracles of intellectual fashion, are rather its belated parrots. Even today, dilettantism pleases them and suits them. If it warps their judgement and corrupts their behaviour, it undeniably gives them an already tarnished but still likeable grace. They make us feel, and even delight in, all the ease and mellowness that existence can provide in highly refined civilizations. Their perpetual embarkation for a spiritual Cythera where the feast would be less one for their blunted senses than for their imaginations, their hearts, their minds, their eyes, their nostrils, and their ears, gives a certain voluptuousness to their postures. The most exact portraitists of this period will not show them, I imagine, looking particularly tense or stiff. Their lives spread the sweet perfume of hair that has been let down.

6

Ambition intoxicates more than fame; desire makes all things blossom, and possession makes them wither away; it is better to dream your life than to live it, even though living it is still dreaming it, albeit less mysteriously and less clearly, in a dark, heavy dream, like the dream diffused through the dim awareness of ruminating beasts. Shakespeare's plays are more beautiful when viewed in a study than when put on in the theatre. The poets who have created imperishable women in love have often only ever known humdrum servant girls from taverns, while the most envied voluptuaries are unable to grasp fully the life they lead, or rather the life which leads *them*. – I knew a young boy of ten, of sickly disposition and precocious imagination, who had developed a purely cerebral love for an older girl. He would stay at his window for hours on end to see her walk by, wept if he didn't see her, wept even more even if he did. He spent moments with her that were very few and far between. He stopped sleeping and eating. One day, he threw himself out of his window. People thought at first that despair at never getting close to his lady friend had filled him with the resolve to die. They learnt that, on the contrary, he had just had a long conversation with her: she had been extremely nice to him. Then people supposed that he had renounced the insipid days he still had to live, after this intoxication that he might never be able to experience again. Frequent remarks he had previously made to one of his friends finally led people to deduce that he was filled with disappointment every time he saw the sovereign lady of his dreams; but as soon as she had left, his fertile imagination restored all her power to the absent girl, and he would start to long for her again. Each time, he would try to find an accidental reason for his disappointment in the imperfect nature of the circumstances. After that final interview in which he had, in his already active and inventive fantasy, raised his lady friend to the high perfection of which her nature was capable, and been filled with despair when he compared that imperfect perfection to the absolute perfection on which he lived and from which he was dying, he threw himself out of the window. Subsequently, having been reduced to idiocy, he lived for a long time, since his fall had left him with no memory of his soul, his mind, or of the words of his lady friend, whom he now met without seeing her. In spite of supplications and threats, she married him, and died several years later, without having managed to make him recognise her. – Life is like this girl. We dream of it, and we love what we have dreamt up. We must not try to live it: we throw ourselves, like that boy, into a state of stupidity – but not all at once: everything in life deteriorates by imperceptible degrees. Within ten years, we do not recognise our dreams, we deny them, we live, like an ox, for the grass we graze on moment by moment. And from our marriage with death, who knows if we will arise as conscious, immortal beings?

7

'Captain,' said his orderly, a few days after the little house had been made ready for him to live in, now that he had retired, until the day he died (a heart disease meant that this would not be long), 'Captain, perhaps now that you can no longer make love, or go into battle, a few books might provide you with some entertainment; what should I go and buy for you?'

'Don't buy anything; no books; they can't tell me anything as interesting as what I've done, and since I don't have long for that, I don't want anything to distract me from remembering it. Give me the key to my big trunk; its contents will give me plenty to read every day.'

And from it he took out letters, a whole sea of letters, flecked with white and sometimes grey in hue. Some of these letters were very long, some of them just a single line, written on cards, with faded flowers, various objects, notes to himself to help him remember what had been going on when he received them, and photographs that had been spoilt despite his precautions, like those relics that the very piety of the faithful has worn away with too frequent kisses. And all of those things were very old, and some of them came from dead women, and others from women he had not seen for over ten years.

In all this there were small things that bore the precise memory of episodes of sensuality or affection fabricated from the most insignificant circumstances in his life, and it was like a vast fresco, depicting his life without narrating it, selecting only its most colourful and passionate moments, in a way at once very vague and very precise, with great and poignant power. There were evocations of kisses on the mouth – that young mouth where he would unhesitatingly have left his soul, and which had since turned away from him: these made him weep for a long time. And despite the fact that he was very weak and forlorn, when he emptied at one draught a few of these still vivid memories, like a glass of warm wine matured in the sunshine that had devoured his life, he felt a nice lukewarm shudder, of the kind spring gives us when we are convalescing, or the winter hearth when it warms our languor. The feeling that his old worn-out body had all the same burned with the same flames gave him a new lease of life – burned with the same devouring flames. Then, reflecting that what was stretching out its full length over him was merely the immense and moving shadow of those things, so elusive, alas! and soon to be mingled together in eternal night, he would start to weep again.

Then, even though he knew that they were only shadows, the shadows of flames that had flickered away to burn elsewhere, and that he would never see them again, he nonetheless started to worship those shadows and to lend them a cherished existence, as it were, in contrast to the absolute nothingness that lay in wait. And all those kisses and all those locks of hair he had kissed and all those things of tears and lips, of caresses poured out like an intoxicating wine, and the moments of despair as vast as music or eventide, filled with the bliss of imagining that they could touch the infinite and its mysterious destinies; this or that adored woman who held him so tightly that nothing existed henceforth except that which he could employ in the service of her adoration… she held him so tightly, and now she was leaving him, becoming so indistinct that he could not hold her back, could no longer even retain the perfume that wafted from the fugitive hems of her mantle: he bent his every effort to reliving it all, trying to bring it back to life and pin it down in front of him like a butterfly. And each time it grew more difficult. And he had still not caught a single one of the butterflies – but each time his fingernails had scratched away a little of the mirage of their wings; or rather, he could see them in a mirror, and banged vainly against the mirror in his attempt to touch them, but merely tarnished it a little each time, so that the butterflies simply became blurred and less enchanting to his eyes. And this mirror of his heart was so tarnished that nothing could wipe it clean any more, now that the purifying breath of youth or genius would no longer blow over it – by what unknown law of our seasons, what mysterious equinox of our autumn?…

And each time, he felt less sorrow at having lost them – those kisses on that mouth, and those endless hours, and those perfumes that once had made him delirious.

And he was filled with sorrow at feeling less sorrow; and even *that* sorrow soon vanished. Then all his sorrows left, every one; no need to send his pleasures packing; they had fled long since on their winged heels, without looking round, holding their flowering branches in their hands; they had fled the dwelling that was no longer young enough for them. Then, like all men, he died.

8

Relics

I have bought up all of her belongings that were put on sale – that woman whose friend I would like to have been, and who did not even condescend to talk to me for a few minutes. I have the little card game that kept her amused every evening, her two marmosets, three novels that bear her coat of arms on their boards, and her bitch. Oh, you delights and dear playthings of her life, you had access – without enjoying them as I would have done, and without even desiring them – to all her freest, most inviolable, and most secret hours; you were unaware of your happiness and you cannot describe it.

Cards that she would hold in her fingers every evening with her favourite friends who saw her getting bored or breaking into laughter, who were witnesses to the start of her liaison, and whom she threw down to fling her arms round the man who thereafter came every evening to enjoy a game with her; novels that she would open and close in her bed, as her fancy or her fatigue bade her, chosen by her on impulse or as her dreams dictated, books to which she confided her dreams and combined them with the dreams expressed by the books that helped her better to dream for herself – did you retain nothing of her, and can you tell me nothing about her?

Novels; she dreamt in turn the lives of your characters and of your authors; and playing cards, for in her own way she enjoyed in your company the tranquillity and sometimes the feverishness of intimate friendships – did you keep nothing of her thoughts, which you distracted or filled, or of her heart, which you wounded or consoled?

Cards, novels, you were so often in her hands, or remained for so long on her table; queens, kings or knaves, who were the still guests at her wildest parties; heroes of novels and heroines who, at her bedside, caught in the cross-beam of her lamp and her eyes, dreamt your silent dream, a dream that was nonetheless filled with voices: you cannot have simply let it evaporate – all the perfume with which the air of her bedroom, the fabric of her dresses, and the touch of her hands or her knees imbued you.

You have preserved the creases left when her joyful or nervous hand crumpled you; you perhaps still keep prisoner those tears which she shed, on reading of a grief narrated in some book, or experienced in life; the day which made her eyes shine with joy or sorrow left its warm hues on you. When I touch you, I shiver, anxiously awaiting your revelations, disquieted by your silence. Alas! perhaps, like you, charming and fragile creatures, she was the insensible and unconscious witness of her own grace. Her most real beauty existed perhaps in my desire. She lived her life, but perhaps I was the only one to dream it.

9

Moonlight sonata

I

I had been worn out less by the fatigues of the journey than by the memory and the apprehension of my father's demands, of Pia's indifference, and of my enemies' relentlessness. During the day, the company of Assunta, her singing, her kindness to me (even though she barely even knew me), her white, brown and pink beauty, her perfume which continued to hang in the great gusts of wind from the sea, the feather in her hat, the pearls around her neck, had taken my mind off those problems. But, around nine in the evening, feeling overwhelmed with fatigue, I asked her to go back in the carriage and leave me here to rest awhile in the open air. We had almost reached Honfleur; the place had been well chosen, against a wall, at the start of a double avenue of great trees which gave shelter from the wind; the air was mild; she agreed, and left me. I lay down on the grass, my face turned towards the dark sky; lulled by the sound of the sea, which I could hear behind me, without being able to see it clearly in the darkness, I had quickly dozed off.

Soon I dreamt that in front of me the sunset was shedding its light on the sand and the sea in the distance. Twilight was falling, and it seemed to me that it was a sunset and a twilight like all twilights and all sunsets.

But a letter was brought to me; I tried to read it and couldn't make anything out. Only then did I realise that in spite of this impression of intense and widespread light, it was in fact very dark. This sunset was extraordinarily wan, glowing without clarity, and on the magically illumined sand, the darkness had become so deep and dense that I had to make an intense effort to recognise the shape of a seashell. In that twilight particular to dreams, it was like the setting of an ailing and discoloured sun, on some polar strand. My sorrows had suddenly evaporated; my father's decisions, Pia's feelings, my enemies' bad faith still held me in their thrall, but they no longer crushed me; it was as if they were a natural and now indifferent necessity. The paradox of this dark gleam, the miracle of this magical truce granted to my problems, inspired no mistrust in me, and no fear – but I was wrapped, bathed, drowned in a growing sweetness whose intense delight finally awoke me. I opened my eyes. In wan splendour, my dream stretched all around me. The wall in whose shelter I had curled up to sleep was brightly lit, and the shadow cast by its ivy fell as clear and vivid as if it had been four in the afternoon. The leaves of a white poplar, quivering in the barely perceptible breeze, glittered. Waves and white sails could be seen on the sea, the sky was clear, the moon had risen. Every so often, light clouds passed in front of it, but then they became tinged with a delicate blue, whose profound pallor was like that of a transparent jellyfish or the heart of an opal. And yet my eyes could nowhere grasp the brightness that was shining all around. Even on the grass, which shone with a mirage-like intensity, the darkness persisted. The woods, or a ditch, were totally black. Suddenly, a slight noise rose as slowly and surely as a growing anxiety, rapidly grew louder, and seemed to come rolling across the wood. It was the rustle of the leaves quivering in the breeze. One by one I heard them unfurling like waves against the vast silence of the huge night sky. Then even this noise diminished and faded away. In the narrow meadow stretching before me between the dense avenues of oak trees, there seemed to flow a river of light, contained within these two riverbanks of shadow. The moonlight, as it summoned forth the gamekeeper's house, the foliage, or a sail from the night in which they lay buried, had not awoken them. In the silence of sleep, it illumined merely the vague phantom of their forms, without it being possible to distinguish the outlines which restored them to me in their full daytime reality, oppressing me then by the certainty of their presence, and the permanency of their banal proximity. The house without a door, the foliage without a trunk and almost without leaves, the sail without a ship, seemed, instead of being a cruelly undeniable and monotonously habitual reality, the strange, inconsistent and luminous dream of the sleeping trees immersed in the darkness. Never, indeed, had the woods slept so deeply; the moon gave the impression of having taken advantage of their slumber to throw a great but subdued party, sweetly spectral, silently unfolding over the sea and the sky. My sadness had vanished. I could hear my father scolding me, Pia making fun of me, my enemies hatching plots – and none of this seemed real. The only reality lay in this unreal light, and I summoned it with a smile. I did not understand what mysterious resemblance had united my sorrows to the solemn mysteries being celebrated in the woods, on the sea and in the sky, but I felt that their explanation, their consolation, their pardon was being proffered, and that it was quite unimportant that my intelligence had been left out of the secret, since my heart understood it so well. I called my holy mother night by name, my sadness had recognised in the moon her immortal sister, the moon shone on the transfigured sufferings of night, and in my heart, whence the clouds had dispersed, there had risen a great melancholy.

II

Then I heard steps. Assunta was coming towards me, her white face hovering over a vast dark mantle. She said to me, almost under her breath, 'I was afraid you might be cold, my brother had gone to bed, I came back.' I went up to her; I was shivering, she took me under her mantle and, to hold it in place, put her arm round my neck. We walked a few steps beneath the trees, in the deep darkness. Something shone in front of us; I did not have time to step back and went round it, thinking we were going to walk into a tree, but the obstacle vanished beneath our feet; we had walked into a pool of moonlight. I leaned her head against mine. She smiled, I started to weep, I saw that she was weeping too. Then we realised that the moon was weeping and that her sadness was in unison with ours. The gentle, poignant accents of her light went straight to our hearts. Like us, she was weeping, and, as is almost always the case with us, she was weeping without knowing why, but feeling her sweet and irresistible despair so deeply that she dragged down into it the woods, the fields, the sky – which was again reflected in the sea – and my heart, which at last could see clearly into hers.

10

The source of tears that are in past loves

The way novelists or their heroes hark back to their defunct love affairs, so touching for the reader, is unfortunately quite artificial. This contrast between the immensity of our past love and the absolute nature of our present indifference, of which a thousand material details make us aware – a name recalled in conversation, a letter discovered lying in a drawer, an actual meeting with the person, or, even more, our belated and, as it were, retrospective possession of that person; this contrast, so painful, so full of barely contained tears when represented in a work of art, is something we can register with frigid detachment in life, precisely because our present state is one of indifference and forgetfulness, because our beloved and our love no long afford us any pleasure other than an aesthetic one at most, and because, together with love, our emotional turmoil and our faculty of suffering have disappeared. The poignant melancholy of this contrast is thus merely a moral truth. It would also become a psychological reality if a writer were to place it at the beginning of the passion he is describing and not after its end.

Indeed, when we begin to love, it is often the case that, forewarned by our experience and our sagacity – despite the protestation of our heart which has the feeling or rather the illusion that its love will last for ever, – we know that one day the woman the thought of whom constitutes our whole life will be as indifferent to us as are, just now, all other women apart from her... We will hear her name without any thrill of pain, we will see her handwriting without trembling, we will not change our route to catch a glimpse of her in the street, we will meet her without being affected by the encounter, we will possess her without ecstasy. Then that sure foreknowledge, despite the absurd and yet powerful premonition that we will always love her, will make us weep; and love, the love that will still be hovering over us like a divine morning, infinitely mysterious and sad, will offer to our pain some of the expanse of its great and strange horizons, in all their depth, and some of its enchanting desolation...

11

Friendship

When we are filled with sorrow, it is sweet to hide in the warmth of our beds and, now that all effort and all resistance have been abandoned, pull our head under the blankets, and completely let ourselves go, groaning like branches in the autumn wind. But there is an even better bed, filled with divine perfumes. It is our sweet, our deep, our impenetrable friendship. When my heart is feeling sad and frozen, I shelter it in our friendship, shivering in the cold. Burying even my thoughts in the warmth of our affection, perceiving nothing more of the world outside and no longer seeking to defend myself, disarmed, but by the miracle of our tender affection immediately fortified, invincible, I weep with pain, and with the joy of having a trusting soul in which I can lock it away.

12

The ephemeral efficacity of sorrow

Let us be grateful to the people who give us happiness; they are the charming gardeners thanks to whom our souls are filled with flowers. But let us be more grateful to the spiteful or merely indifferent women, and to the cruel friends who have caused us sorrow. They have laid waste to our hearts that are now strewn with unrecognisable debris, they have uprooted the trunks and mutilated the most delicate branches, like a desolate wind, but one which sowed a few good seeds in the uncertain hope of some future harvest.

These people have, by breaking to pieces all the brief moments of happiness that concealed the extent of our misery from us, and by turning our heart into a naked and melancholy courtyard, made it possible for us to contemplate our heart and judge it. Plays with sad endings do us good in a similar way; so we should consider them as greatly superior to plays that end happily, which cheat our hunger rather than satisfying it: the bread from which we must draw sustenance is bitter to the taste. When life is going well, the destinies of our fellows do not appear to us in their reality, since either interest masks them or desire transfigures them. But in the detachment afforded by suffering (in life), and in the feeling of a painful beauty (in the theatre), the destinies of other men, and ours too, force our attentive souls to hear at last the eternal unheard message of duty and truth. The sad oeuvre of a real artist speaks to us with the accent of those who have suffered and who force every man who has suffered to drop everything else and listen.

Alas! our feelings brought these insights to us and our capricious feelings take them away: sadness, a higher quality than gaiety, is not as enduring as virtue. This morning we have already forgotten the tragedy which last night elevated us so high that we were able to view our life as a whole and as a reality, with a clear-sighted and sincere pity. After just a year, perhaps, we will be consoled for the betrayal of a woman or the death of a friend. The wind, amidst this flotsam of dreams, this scattered chaos of withered joys, has sown the good seed and watered it with tears, but those tears will dry too quickly for it ever to germinate.

(After *L'Invitée* by M. de Curel[12])

13

In praise of bad music

Detest bad music if you will, but don't despise it. As it is played and sung much more often and much more passionately than good music, so much more than the latter has it gradually been filled with the dreams and tears of mankind. For that reason you should venerate it. Its place, insignificant in the history of art, is huge in the sentimental history of societies. Respect for – I do not say love for – bad music is not merely a form of what might be called the charity of good taste or its scepticism, it is, more than that, the awareness of the importance of the social role of music. How many melodies, worthless in the eyes of an artist, become the confidants chosen by a whole host of romantic young men and of women in love. How many 'golden rings' and 'Ah! sleep on, sleep on, mistress mine', the pages of which are tremulously turned every evening by justly celebrated hands, and watered by the most beautiful eyes in the world with tears whose melancholy and voluptuous tribute would arouse the envy of the most stringent maestro in the world, – ingenious and inspired confidants who ennoble sorrow and exalt dreams, and, in exchange for the ardent secret confided to them, give the intoxicating illusion of beauty. The working classes, the bourgeoisie, the army, the nobility, just as they have the same postmen to bring news of some grief to afflict them with sorrow or some happiness to fill them with pleasure, have the same invisible messengers of love, and the same cherished confessors – in other words, bad musicians. The irritating refrain, for instance, that any refined and well-trained ear will immediately refuse to listen to, has been the repository for the riches of thousands of souls, and keeps the secret of thousands of lives, for which it was the living inspiration, the ever-ready consolation, always lying half-open on the piano's music stand – a source of dreamy grace for those lives, and an ideal. Those arpeggios too, or that 're-entry' of the theme, have aroused in the soul of more than one lover or dreamer an echo of the harmonies of paradise or the very voice of the beloved woman. A book of bad romances, worn out by over-use, ought to touch us like a cemetery or a village. What does it matter if the houses have no style, if the tombs are overladen with inscriptions and ornaments in bad taste? From this dust there may arise, in the eyes of an imagination friendly and respectful enough to silence for a moment its aesthetic disdain, the flock of souls holding in their beaks the still verdant dream that gave them a foretaste of the other world and filled them with joy or tears in this one.

14

A meeting by the lakeside

Yesterday, before going to have dinner in the Bois, I received a letter from Her – a rather frigid reply, a week after I had sent her a despairing letter, to say that she was afraid she would not be able to bid me farewell before leaving. And I, quite frigidly, yes, I replied to her that it was better like that and that I wished her a pleasant summer. Then I got dressed and crossed the Bois in an open carriage. I was extremely sad, but calm. I was resolved to forget, my mind was made up: it was just a matter of time.

As the carriage moved down the avenue to the lake, I spotted at the very far end of the little path that goes round the lake, fifty metres from the avenue, a solitary woman walking slowly along. I did not at first make her out clearly. She gave me a little wave, and then I recognised her in spite of the distance between us. It was her! I gave her a long slow wave. And she continued to gaze at me as if she had wished to see me stop and take her with me. I did nothing of the kind, but I soon felt an emotion seizing on me as if from some external source and holding me tightly in its grip. 'I *knew* it!' I exclaimed to myself. 'There is a reason unknown to me which has always led her to pretend to be indifferent. She loves me, the little darling!' A boundless happiness and an invincible certainty overwhelmed me; I felt as if I would faint, and I burst into tears. The carriage was approaching Armenonville, I wiped my eyes and over them passed, as if to dry their tears, the sweet wave of her hand, and her gently questioning eyes gazed steadfastly on mine, asking to get into the carriage with me.

I arrived at the dinner in a radiant mood. My happiness overflowed on everyone in the form of a joyous, grateful and cordial affability; and the feeling that none of them knew what hand, unknown to them (the little hand that had waved to me) had lit within me that great fire of joy whose blaze everyone could see – this feeling imbued my happiness with the added charm of a secret pleasure. We were waiting only for Mme de T*** and she soon arrived. She is the most insignificant person I know, and despite quite a good figure, the least likeable. But I was too happy not to forgive each of her failings and her ugliness, and I went up to her with an affectionate smile.

'You weren't so friendly just now,' she said.

'Just now?' I said in astonishment. 'Just now? But I didn't see you.'

'What – you didn't recognise me? It's true you were some way away; I was walking by the lakeside, you passed proudly by in your carriage, I waved to you and I would really rather have liked to get into your carriage so as not to be late.'

'Oh, it was you!' I exclaimed, and I added several times with an expression of great sorrow, 'Oh, please forgive me! Please forgive me!'

'How unhappy he looks! My compliments, Charlotte,' said the hostess. 'But cheer up, young man, you're with her now!'

I was devastated; my happiness had been totally destroyed.

Well, the most horrible thing about my mistake was that it refused to go away. That loving image of the woman who no longer loved me, changed for a good long while my idea of her even once I had recognised my error. I tried to patch it up between us, I took longer to forget her, and often, in my pain, to try and console myself by forcing myself to believe that those hands had, as I'd at first *sensed*, belonged to her, I would close my eyes to see again her little hands waving to me, hands that would so would so nicely have wiped away my tears, and cooled my brow, her little gloved hands that she gently held out to me by the lakeside like frail symbols of peace, love and reconciliation while her sad, questioning eyes seemed to be asking me to take her with me.

15

Just as a blood-red sky warns the passer-by that there is a fire in the distance, certain fiery glances, of course, can betray passions that they serve merely to reflect. They are flames in the mirror. But sometimes, as well, indifferent and cheerful people have eyes as vast and sombre as sorrows, as if a filter were held out between their souls and their eyes and as if they had so to speak 'filtered' all the living content of their soul into their eyes. Henceforth, warmed only by the fervour of their egotism – that likeable fervour of egotism which attracts others just as much as incendiary passion repels them – their shrivelled souls will be little more than a factitious palace of intrigue. But their eyes, ceaselessly inflamed with love, and soon to be moistened with the dew of languor that will make them gleam, swim and drown, without being able to extinguish them – their eyes will amaze the universe with their tragic blaze. Twin spheres, henceforth independent of their soul, spheres of love, burning satellites of a world that has frozen over forever, they will continue until their death to cast an unwonted and deceptive gleam, false prophets, and perjurers too, promising a love with which their heart will not keep faith.

16

The stranger

Dominique had sat near the now extinguished fire as he waited for his guests. Every evening, he would invite some great lord to come and dine with him, together with some witty guests, and as he was well born, rich and charming, he was never alone. The candles had not yet been lit and the day was fading away in the melancholy gloom of the bedroom. Suddenly, he heard a voice addressing him, a distant and intimate voice saying, 'Dominique'; and merely hearing it uttered, uttered so far away and so near – 'Dominique' – he was frozen by fear. Never before had he heard that voice, and yet he recognised it so easily; his remorse recognised so clearly the voice of a victim, a noble sacrificial victim. He tried to think what old crime he had committed, and could not remember. And yet the tone of this voice was certainly reproaching him with a crime, a crime that he had doubtless committed without being aware of it, but for which he was responsible – this much was attested by his sadness and his fear. – He looked up and saw, standing in front of him, grave and familiar, a stranger of ambiguous but striking aspect. Dominique greeted his melancholy and undeniable authority with a few respectful words.

'Dominique, could I be the only man you will not invite to dinner? You committed crimes against me, old crimes, and you need to make reparation for them. And then I will teach you to get by without other people who, when you are old, will come no more.'

'I *do* invite you to dinner,' replied Dominique with an affectionate gravity that he had never suspected in himself.

'Thank you,' said the stranger.

There were no insignia inscribed in the gemstone on his ring, and wit had not glazed his words with the brilliant needles of its hoar frost. But the gratitude in his steady, fraternal gaze filled Dominique with an unfamiliar and intoxicating happiness.

'But if you wish to keep me with you, you must send away your other guests.'

Dominique could hear them knocking at the door. The candles had not been lit, the darkness was complete.

'I can't send them away,' said Dominique, '*I can't be alone.*'

'And with me, you would indeed be alone,' said the stranger, sadly. 'And yet you really should keep me. You committed old crimes against me and you need to make reparation for them. I love you more than do any of the others, and I would teach you to get by without them, for, when you are old, they will come no more.'

'I can't,' said Dominique.

And he sensed that he had just sacrificed a noble happiness, following the orders of some imperious and vulgar habit, which no longer even had any pleasures to dispense to him in reward for obedience.

'Choose quickly,' resumed the stranger, in a suppliant and haughty tone.

Dominique went to open the door to the guests, and at the same time he asked the stranger, without daring to turn his head:

'So who are you?'

And the stranger, the stranger who was already starting to vanish, told him:

'The habit to which you are sacrificing me again this evening will be even stronger tomorrow thanks to the blood from the wound that you are inflicting on me to nourish it. More imperious for having been obeyed one more time, each day it will turn you away from me, will force you to make me suffer even more. Soon you will have killed me. You will never see me again. And yet you owed more to me than to the others, who, very shortly, will abandon you. I am within you and yet I am forever far away from you; already I barely exist any more. I am your soul, I am yourself.'

The guests had come in. They passed into the dinner room and Dominique tried to relate his conversation with the vanished visitor, but given the general boredom, and the visible effort the host was forced to make in trying to recall an almost faded dream, Girolamo interrupted him, to the satisfaction of all, including Dominique himself, and drew this conclusion:

'One should never remain alone – solitude engenders melancholy.'

Then they started drinking again; Dominique chatted gaily but joylessly, flattered, nonetheless, by his brilliant guests.

17

Dream

> *Your tears flowed for me, my lips have drunk your tears.*
> (Anatole France)

I can effortlessly remember what my opinion of Mme Dorothy B*** was last Saturday (four days ago). As chance would have it, it was on that very day that people had been talking about her, and I was sincere when I said that I found her without charm or wit. I think she is twenty-two or twenty-three. In addition I hardly really know her, and when I was thinking about her, no vivid memory rose to the surface of my attention; I merely had the letters of her name before my eyes.

On Saturday I went to bed quite early. But at around two o'clock the wind became so strong that I was forced to get up again to close a loose shutter that had woken me up. I cast a retrospective glance over the short period in which I had just been sleeping, a retrospective glance and was delighted to see how restorative it had been, without discomfort or dreams. Hardly had I climbed back into bed than I was again asleep. But after a certain while, it was difficult to say precisely how long, little by little I awoke, or rather I woke little by little into the world of dreams, indistinct, at first, just like the real world when we wake up in the ordinary fashion; but it soon became more precise. I was lying on the beach at Trouville, which was simultaneously a hammock in an unfamiliar garden, and a woman was gazing at me with a fixed and gentle expression. It was Mme Dorothy B***. I was no more surprised than I am in the morning, when I wake up and recognise my bedroom. But nor was I surprised at the supernatural allure of my companion and the transports of simultaneously sensual and spiritual adoration that her presence aroused in me. We gazed at each other in mutual understanding, and a great miracle of happiness and glory was in the process of being accomplished, a miracle of which we were fully conscious, for which she bore a shared responsibility, and for which I was infinitely grateful to her. But she was saying to me:

'You are crazy to thank me – wouldn't you have done the same thing for me?'

And the feeling (in fact, it was a sense of perfect certainty) that I would indeed have done the same thing for her exalted my joy to the point of delirium, like the manifest symbol of the closest union. She made a mysterious sign with her finger, and smiled. And I knew, as if I had been both within myself and within her, that it meant, 'All your enemies, all your problems, all your regrets, all your weaknesses – are they now quite gone?' And without my having said a word, she heard me replying to her that she had easily been victorious over everything, had destroyed everything, and most pleasurably mesmerised my suffering away. And she approached, stroking my neck, and gently playing with the tips of my moustache. Then she said to me, 'Now let us go to the others, let us enter into life.' A superhuman joy filled me, and I felt within myself the strength to realise this virtual happiness in its entirety. She wanted to give me a flower, and from between her breasts she drew a rose whose bud was still closed, yellow and bedewed, and attached it to my buttonhole. Suddenly, I felt my intoxication increased by a new pleasure. It was the rose which, fixed to my buttonhole, had started to exhale its odour of love into my nostrils. I saw that Dorothy was disturbed by my joy and filled with an emotion that I could not understand. At the very same moment as her eyes (and I was certain of this, thanks to the mysterious awareness I had of her own individuality) experienced the slight spasm that precedes by a single second the moment when one starts to weep, it was my eyes which filled with tears – with her tears, I might almost say. She came up to me, placed her head to my cheek, throwing it back so that I could contemplate its mysterious grace, its captivating viv-aciousness, and darting out her tongue from her young, smiling mouth, gathered all my tears on the edges of my eyes. Then she swallowed them, making a slight noise with her lips, which I experienced as a strange new kiss, more intimately disturbing than if it had touched me directly. I suddenly awoke, recognised my bedroom and just as, when a storm is close, a clap of thunder follows immediately after the flash of lightning, a dizzy memory of happiness coincided with, rather than preceding, the crushing certainty of its falseness and impossibility. But, in spite of all rational argument, Dorothy B*** had ceased to be for me the woman she had still been the day before. The little furrow left in my memory by the few occasions on which I had met her had almost been effaced, as after a powerful tide which had left unfamiliar traces behind it as it withdrew. I had a huge desire, disappointed in advance, to see her again, and an instinctive need to write to her, restrained by a cautious mistrust. Her name uttered in a conversation made me start, and yet merely evoked the insignificant image that would alone have accompanied her name before that night; and while she was a matter of indifference to me just like any other ordinary society woman, she attracted me more irresistibly than the most beloved mistresses, or the most intoxicating destiny. I would not have taken a single step to see her, and yet for the other 'her' I would have given my life. Every hour effaces something of the memory of this dream that is already quite disfigured by my relating it. I can see it less and less distinctly, like a book that you want to carry on reading at your table when the declining day no longer sheds enough light, when night falls. If I wish still to perceive it, I am obliged to stop thinking about it for a few minutes, just as you are obliged to close your eyes at first if you are to continue to read a few letters in the book filled with shadow. However much it has been effaced, it still leaves a great turmoil within me, the foam of its wake or the sensuality of its perfume. But this turmoil itself will vanish, and I will see Mme B*** without it bothering me. And anyway, what would be the use of talking to her about these things, of which she has remained quite unaware?

Alas! love has passed over me like this dream, with a power of transfiguration just as mysterious. And so, you who know the woman I love, and who were not part of my dream, you cannot understand me – so do not try to give me any advice.

18

The genre paintings of memory

We have certain memories that are, as it were, the Dutch paintings of our memory, genre pictures in which the characters are often of the middling sort, taken at a perfectly ordinary moment of their lives, without any solemn events, sometimes without any events at all, in a setting that is in no way extraordinary and quite lacking in grandeur. The natural quality of the characters and the innocence of the scene are what comprise its attractiveness, and distance sets between it and us a gentle light which bathes it in beauty.

My regimental life was full of scenes of this kind that I experienced quite naturally, without any particularly intense joy and without any deep sorrow, and which I remember with much gentle affection. The rural character of the location, the simplicity of some of my peasant comrades, whose bodies had remained more handsome and more agile, their minds more original, their hearts more spontaneous, and their characters more natural than was the case with the young men I frequented previously as well as subsequently, the calm of a life in which one's occupations are more regular and imagination less enslaved than in any other, in which pleasure keeps us company all the more continually as we never have the time to flee from it by running after it – everything concurs to make, now, of this period of my life a series (admittedly filled with gaps) of little paintings imbued with charm and a truth bathed in happiness, on which time has shed its sweet sadness and its poetry.

19

Sea breeze in the countryside

> *I will bring you a young poppy, with crimson petals.*
> (Theocritus, *The Cyclops*)

In the garden, in the little wood, across the countryside, the wind deploys a crazed and futile ardour in scattering the flurries of sunlight, harrying them along as it furiously shakes the branches of the coppice where they had first flung themselves, all the way to the sparkling thicket where they now tremble, all aquiver. Trees, clothes hanging out to dry, the outspread tail of the peacock, all cast, through the transparent air, extraordinarily clear blue shadows that fly along before every gust of wind without leaving the ground, like a kite that has not taken off. The helter-skelter of wind and light makes this nook of the Champagne region resemble a coastal landscape. When we reach the top of this path which, scorched by the light and swept by the wind, climbs up in the dazzling sunlight, towards a naked sky, is it not the sea that will soon greet our sight, white with sunlight and foam? In the same way, you had come every morning, your hands filled with flowers and the soft feathers which a wood pigeon, a swallow or a jay had dropped onto the avenue as it flew past. The feathers tremble in my hat, the poppy in my buttonhole is shedding its petals, let's go home, this very minute.

The house groans in the wind like a ship, you can hear invisible sails bellying out and invisible flags cracking outside. Let this clump of fresh roses continue to lie across your knees and allow my heart to weep between your clasped hands.

20

The pearls

I came home as day was dawning and, shivering in the cold, went to bed, all aquiver with a melancholy and frozen frenzy. Just a while ago, in your room, your friends from the day before, your plans for the next day (so many enemies, so many plots being hatched against me), and your current thoughts (so many hazy miles I would never be able to cross) separated you from me. Now that I am far away from you, this imperfect presence, the fleeting mask of eternal absence (a mask which kisses soon lift) would, it seems to me, be enough to show me your true face and to fulfil every aspiration of my love. I had to take my leave; how sad and frozen I remain when far from you! But by what sudden enchantment do the familiar dreams of our happiness again start to rise up, a thick smoke mounting from a clear and burning flame, climbing joyfully and uninterruptedly in my head? From my closed hand, as it warms up beneath the blankets, there again wafts the odour of the rose cigarettes that you had given me to smoke. I plant my lips on my hand and draw in, deeply and slowly, the perfume which, in the heat of memory, breathes out dense whiffs of tenderness, of happiness, of 'you'. Ah, my beloved! At the very same moment that I can so easily do without you, as I wallow joyfully in your memory – which now fills the bedroom – without having to struggle against your insurmountable body, let me tell you, absurd as it is, let me tell you, for I cannot help it, that I cannot do without you. It is your presence which imparts to my life that subtle hue, warm and melancholy, with which it also imbues the pearls that spend the night on your body. Like them, I live on your warmth and sorrowfully take on its subtle tints, and like them, if you did not keep me on you, I would die.

2 1

The shores of oblivion

'They say that Death makes beautiful those whom it strikes down, and exaggerates their virtues, but in general it is much truer to say that it was life that failed to do them justice. Death, that pious and irreproachable witness, teaches us, in accordance with truth and love, that in every person there is usually more good than evil.' What Michelet here says about death is perhaps even truer of that death which follows a great unhappy love affair. Take a person who, after making us suffer so much, ceases to mean anything at all to us – is it enough to say, as does the common expression, that such a person is 'dead for us'? We weep for the dead, we still love them, for a long time we are subject to the irresistible attraction of the enchantment that survives them and which often causes us to return to their tombs. But the person who has made us feel every emotion, and by whose essence we are saturated, can no longer even cast on us the merest shadow of any sorrow or joy. Such a person is more than dead for us. After considering such a person as the sole thing of value in this world, after cursing him and despising him, we find it impossible to judge him, the features of his face are barely discernible to the eyes of our memory, exhausted as they are by having gazed on him for too long. But this judgement on the loved one, a judgement which varied so considerably, sometimes torturing our blind hearts with its sharp eyes, sometimes itself turning a blind eye to any failings so as to overcome the cruel discord, must undergo one last swing of the pendulum. Like those landscapes which are revealed to us only when we have reached the summit, from the heights of forgiveness there appears in her true value the woman who was more than dead for us, having once been our life itself. We knew only that she did not return our love, we understand now that she felt real friendship for us. It is not memory which makes her more beautiful, it was love which failed to do her justice. To the man who wants everything, and to whom even everything, were he to obtain it, would not suffice, to receive but a little appears as no more than a cruel absurdity. Now we understand that it was a generous gift from her whom our despair, our irony, and our perpetual tyranny had not disheartened. She was always kind. Several of her remarks, mentioned to us only today, strike us as indulgently exact and full of charm – remarks made by the woman we thought incapable of understanding us because she did not love us. Whereas we spoke about her with so much unfair egotism and severity. In any case, do we not owe her so many things? If that great tide of love has withdrawn forever, nonetheless, when we take a walk within ourselves, we can pick up strange and magical shells and, raising them to our ears, hear with melancholy pleasure and without any pain, the vast roar of bygone days. Then we dwell, with a sudden feeling of tenderness, on the woman who, as our ill fortune would have it, was loved more than she loved. She is no longer 'more than dead' for us. She is a dead woman, whom we remember with affection. Justice requires us to redress the idea we had of her. And by the powerful virtue of justice, she is raised in spirit within our hearts, to appear before that last judgement which we deliver far from her, tranquilly, our eyes filled with tears.

22

Real presence

We loved each other in a remote village of the Engadine, with a name of twofold sweetness: the dreaminess of its German sonority faded into the sensuousness of the Italian syllables. All around, three lakes of a mysterious green bathed forests of pine trees. Glaciers and peaks barred the horizon. In the evening, the diversity of perspectives made the effects of light so varied and gentle. Will we ever forget the strolls by the lake of Sils-Maria, as the afternoon drew to its close, at six o'clock?

The larches, so black in their serenity when set against the dazzling snow, held out towards the pale blue, almost mauve water their branches of soft and shining green. One evening the hour was particularly propitious to us; in a few moments, the sun, as it sank, made the water pass through every hue and our souls partake of every successive delight. Suddenly we made a movement, we had just seen a little pink butterfly, then two, then five, leaving the flowers on our shore and flutter over the lake. Soon they seemed an impalpable haze of pink as they swept away; then they reached the flowers on the far shore, and returned, recommencing their hazardous crossing, sometimes hovering as if tempted by the lake's wonderful and subtle tints, like those of a great fading flower. It was too much for us, and our eyes filled with tears. These little butterflies, as they crossed the lake, passed to and fro across our souls – our souls, quivering with emotion at the sight of such varied beauty, ready to vibrate – passed to and fro like the bow of a sweet violin. The lightness of their flight did not graze the waters, but caressed our eyes and our hearts, and at each beat of their little pink wings we felt faint. When we saw them coming back from the far shore, thereby revealing that they were playing, and taking their pleasure as they floated across the waters, we could hear a delightful harmony; meanwhile, they gradually came back, taking a thousand whimsical detours that varied the original harmony and drew the outline of a melody filled with magical fantasy. Our souls, like sounding boards, could hear in their silent flight a music of enchantment and liberty and all the gentle intense harmonies of the lake, the woods, the sky and our lives accompanied it with a sweet magic that made us dissolve in tears.

I had never spoken to you and you were indeed far from my eyes that year. But how much we loved each other at that time, in the Engadine! Never could I get enough of you, never would I leave you at home. You accompanied me in my walks, you ate at my table, you slept in my bed, you dreamed in my soul. One day – can it be that some sure instinct, some mysterious messenger, never alerted you to those childish amusements with which you were so closely associated, and which you lived through, yes, truly lived through, so much did you have within me a 'real presence'? – one day (neither of us had seen Italy), we were as if thunderstruck by these words which someone said about the Alpgrun:

'From there you can see right into Italy'. We set off for the Alpgrun, imagining that, in the spectacle laid out before the peak, just where Italy started, the harsh reality of the landscape would suddenly end and that, against a dreamlike background, a deep blue valley would open up. On our way, we reminded ourselves that a frontier does not alter the terrain and that even if it did, it would happen so imperceptibly that we would be unable to notice it easily or all at once. Somewhat disappointed, we nonetheless laughed at having been so childish a few moments before.

But when we reached the summit, we were dazzled. Our childlike imaginings had come true before our very eyes. At our side, glaciers sparkled. At our feet, torrents zigzagged down a wild, dark green Engadine landscape. Then there was a rather mysterious hill; and after that, mauve slopes afforded and then withheld glimpses into a real, blue land, a sparkling avenue stretching towards Italy. The names were no longer the same, and immediately harmonised with this new soft sweetness. Someone pointed out the lake of Poschiavo, Pizzo di Verona, the Val di Viola. Then, we went to an extraordinarily wild and solitary spot, where the desolation of nature and the certainty that we were here inaccessible to everyone, invisible and invincible too, would have heightened to a frenzy the pleasure of loving each other in that very place. Then I plumbed the depths of my sadness at not having you with me in your material species, other than enrobed in my nostalgia, in the reality of my desire. I went down some way as far as the place, at a still high altitude, where travellers came to take in the view. In an isolated hostel there is a book in which they write their names. I wrote mine and, next to it, a combination of letters that was an allusion to yours, since just then I found it impossible not to provide myself with some material proof of the reality of your spiritual closeness. By putting something of you into this book it seemed to me that I was relieving myself to a corresponding degree of the obsessive weight under which you were suffocating my soul. And then, I had the immense hope of taking you there one day, to read those lines; and then you would climb even higher with me, to avenge me for all that sadness. Without my having to tell you anything about it, you would have understood everything, or rather you would have remembered it all; and you would let yourself go as you climbed up, leaning on me a little so that I could feel more fully that this time you were really there; and I, between your lips with their slight but persistent savour of your Oriental cigarettes, I would find perfect oblivion. We would utter senseless words aloud, just for the sake of shouting without anyone in the far distance being able to hear us; tufts of short grass, in the gentle breeze of the heights, would quiver alone. The ascent would make you slow down your steps and get rather breathless, and my face would draw near so that I could feel your breath: we would be quite ecstatic. We would also go to where a white lake lies next to a black lake as snugly as a white pearl lies next to a black one. How deeply we would have loved one another in an isolated village of the Engadine! We would have let only mountain guides near us – those men who are so tall and whose eyes reflect things that are not seen by the eyes of other men and are as it were of a different 'water'. But I no longer care about you. Satiety came before possession. Platonic love itself has its points of saturation. I would no longer like to take you to this country which, without understanding or even knowing it, you evoke for me with such a touching fidelity. The sight of you preserves but one charm for me, that of reminding me all at once of those names with their strange sweetness, both German and Italian: Sils-Maria, Silva Plana, Crestalta, Samaden, Celerina, Juliers, Val di Viola.

23

An interior sunset

Like nature, intelligence offers us an array of sights. Never have sunsets or moonlit nights, which have often made me melt into a frenzy of tears, surpassed in the passionate outburst of tenderness they provoke in me that vast and melancholy blaze which, during my walks at the end of the day, then casts its hues on the waves in our soul, as numerous as those the setting sun makes shine on the sea. Then we press on more quickly through the gathering night. More than a knight filled with intoxication and giddiness by the accelerating speed of his adored mount, we yield trembling with trust and joy to the tumultuous thoughts which we feel hold us in their thrall more and more irresistibly the more we possess them and can direct them. Filled with affectionate emotion we make our way through the dark countryside and greet the oaks filled with night, like the solemn field, like the epic witnesses of the momentum that impels us forward and fills us with rapture. On looking up skywards, we cannot fail to recognise, exultantly, in the gaps between the clouds still touched by the sun's farewell, the mysterious reflection of our thoughts: we plunge deeper and deeper into the countryside, and the dog which follows us, the horse which carries us, or the now silent friend (less, at times, when there is no living creature with us), the flower in our buttonholes or the walking stick waved about joyfully by our feverish hands, receive in glances and tears the melancholy tribute of our frenzy.

24

As by moonlight

Night had fallen; I went to my room, now too filled with anxiety to remain in the dark without seeing the sky, the fields and the sea gleaming in the sunlight. But when I opened the door, I found the room lit as if by the setting sun. Through the window I could see the house, the fields, the sky and the sea, or rather it seemed to me as if I could 'see' them again in a dream; the gentle moon reminded me of them rather than showing them to me, shedding over their outlines a pale splendour which did not scatter the darkness that lay as dense as oblivion over their shapes. And I spent hours gazing into the courtyard at the memory, mute, vague, enchanted and pallid, of the things which, during the daytime, had given me pleasure or pain, with their cries, their voices or their persistent hum.

Love has faded, I feel afraid at the threshold of oblivion. But here, tranquil now, a little pale, quite close to me and yet distant and already vague, as if in the moonlight, are all my past times of happiness and all my healed sorrows, gazing at me wordlessly. Their silence fills me with affection while their distance and their wavering pallor intoxicate me with sadness and poetry. And I cannot stop gazing at this interior moonlight.

25

A critique of hope in the light of love

Hardly has an as yet future hour become the present for us than it is divested of its charms, only to recover them, it is true – if our soul is wide and deep enough and able to arrange a fine set of perspective views – when we have left it far behind us, on the roads of memory. Thus the poetic village, towards which we were spurring on our impatient hopes and our weary mares, once again breathes (as soon as we have passed the hill) those veiled harmonies, whose promises the vulgarity of its streets, the jumble of its houses – brought so close together that they flowed into one another on the horizon – and the lifting of the blue mist that seemed to imbue it, had all belied. But like the alchemist, who attributes each of his failures to an accidental cause (a different one each time), far from suspecting an incurable imperfection in the very essence of the present, we accuse the malignity of particular circumstances, the responsibilities of this or that envied position, the bad character of this or that desired mistress, the poor state of our health on a day which was to have been a day of pleasure, or the bad weather or the bad hostelries on our journey, of having poisoned our happiness. Thus, certain that we will manage to eliminate these causes that destroy all fruition, we ceaselessly appeal, with an at times muted but never entirely disillusioned confidence, from a realised (that is, disappointed) dream to a dreamt-of future.

But certain reflective and sorrowful men, even more radiant than others with the light of hope, discover rather quickly that, alas! this light does not gleam at the hours when we expect it, but emanates from our hearts overflowing with rays that are unbeknown to nature and which pour them out in torrents over hope without managing to kindle any fire. These men no longer feel the strength to desire what they know not to be desirable, or to wish to fulfil dreams that will wither in their hearts as soon as they try to pluck them outside themselves. This melancholy predisposition is singularly strengthened and justified in love. Imagination, as it ceaselessly and repeatedly goes over its hopes, wonderfully sharpens its disappointments. Unhappy love, which makes it impossible for us to experience happiness, also prevents us from discovering how null and void that happiness is. But what lesson of philosophy, what advice of old age, what foiled ambition can surpass in melancholy the joys of a happy love affair? You love me, my darling girl; how could you have been so cruel as to tell me? So *that* is the ardent happiness of shared love, the mere thought of which made me feel giddy and my teeth chatter!

I undo your flowers, I lift your hair, I tear off your jewels, I touch your flesh, my kisses cover your body as tumultuously as the rising sea beating against the sand; but you yourself elude me, and with you goes happiness. I have to leave you, I return home alone and sadder. Accusing this latest calamity, I return to you forever; it is my last illusion which I have torn down, I am doomed to unhappiness forever.

I do not know how I had the courage to tell you this, it is the happiness of my whole life that I have just pitilessly rejected, or at least my life's consolation, since your eyes, whose trusting happiness still sometimes filled me with intoxication, will now no longer reflect anything but the sad disenchantment of which your sagacity and your disappointments had already warned you. Since this secret, which one of us was keeping hidden from the other, has now been uttered aloud, there is no longer any happiness for us. We no longer even have the disinterested joys of hope. Hope is an act of faith. We have disabused its credulity: it is dead. Having abandoned the quest for fulfilment and pleasure, we can no longer derive any enchantment from hoping. Hoping without hope, which would be so wise, is impossible.

But come to me, my darling girl. Wipe your eyes, just to see… I don't know if it is tears which are blurring my view, but I think I can make out over there, behind us, great fires being lit. Oh, my darling, how I love you! Give me your hand, let us go towards those lovely fires, but not too close… I think that it is indulgent and mighty Memory which wishes us well and is at this very moment doing so much for us, my dear.

Undergrowth

We have nothing to fear, but much to learn from the vigorous and pacific tribe of trees which endlessly produces for us fortifying essences and tranquillising balms, and in whose graceful company we spend so many fresh, silent and enclosed hours. During those scorching afternoons when the light, by its very excess, evades our gaze, let us go down into one of the Normandy 'estates' from which rise supple, tall and thick-leaved beeches, whose foliage parts that ocean of light like a slender but sturdy barge, and retain of it no more than a few drops that tinkle melodiously in the black silence of the undergrowth. Our spirit does not experience, as it does by the seaside, in the plains, or on the mountains, the joy of spreading over the world, but the happiness of being separated from it; and, hemmed in on every side by trunks that can never be uprooted, it flings itself upwards as do the trees. Lying on our backs, our heads resting on the dry leaves, we can follow from the depths of our deep repose the joyful agility of our spirit mounting, without causing the foliage to tremble, to the highest branches where it settles at the edge of the gentle sky, next to a singing bird. Here and there, a patch of sunlight stagnates at the foot of the trees which, at times, dreamily dangle, in the golden light, the leaves on the tips of their branches. Everything else, relaxed and immobile, remains silent, in a sombre bliss. Soaring and erect, amid the vast offering of their branches, and yet rested and calm, the trees, through their strange and natural posture, invite us with grateful murmurs to feel kinship with a life so ancient and so young, so different from ours and yet appearing as its dark and inexhaustible reservoir.

A light breeze momentarily disturbs their brightly flickering but sombre immobility, and the trees tremble slightly, balancing the light on their tops and stirring the shadows at their feet.

– Petit-Abbeville (Dieppe), August 1895

The chestnut trees

In particular, I loved to pause under the huge chestnut trees when they were turning yellow in the autumn. How many hours I spent in those mysterious green-hued grottoes, gazing at the murmuring cascades of pale gold over my head, as they poured out freshness and darkness! I envied the robins and the squirrels who could live in those frail and deep pavilions of verdure amid the branches, those ancient hanging gardens which each springtime, for two centuries now, has covered with white, sweet-smelling flowers. The branches, imperceptibly curved, swept nobly down from the tree to the ground, as if they were other trees planted into the trunks, upside down. The pallor of the remaining leaves set off even more strongly the branches that already appeared solider and blacker now that they were bare, and attached to the trunk in this way, they seemed to hold in place, like some magnificent comb, the lovely profusion of sweet blond hair.

– Réveillon, October 1895

28

The sea

The sea will always fascinate those for whom world-weariness and the lure of mystery preceded their first sorrows, like a foretaste of reality's inability to satisfy them. Those who need rest even before they have experienced any fatigue will derive consolation from the sea, and a vague sense of exaltation. Unlike the earth, the sea bares no trace of the labours of man and of human life. Nothing remains on it, nothing passes by except fleetingly, and of the ships that cross it, how quickly the wake vanishes! Hence the great purity of the sea, which earthly things do not possess. And that virgin water is much more delicate than the hardened earth, which you need a pickaxe to break open. A child stepping into water makes a deep, hollow furrow in it, accompanied by a bright 'plop!', and the smooth gradations of the water are for a moment broken; then every vestige is effaced, and the sea is again as calm as it was in the first days of the world. He who is weary of the earth's paths or who guesses, after trying them out, how uneven and unrewarding they are, will be seduced by the pale sea roads, more dangerous and more gentle, uncertain and deserted. Everything here is more mysterious, including those great shadows that sometimes peacefully float on the bare fields of the sea, without home and without shelter, cast by the clouds, those hamlets of the skies, those vague branches.

The sea has the allure of things that do not fall silent at night-time, and grant our unquiet lives permission to sleep; a promise that everything is not doomed to disappear forever, like the nightlife of small children who feel less lonely when it glimmers. The sea is not separated from the sky as is the earth; the sea is always in harmony with the sky's colours, and affected by its most delicate tints. The sea gleams in the sunlight, and every evening she seems to die with him. And when the sun has disappeared, she continues to miss him, to preserve something of his glowing memory, unlike the earth which is dark all over. This is the time when her melancholy reflections gleam, so sweet that you feel your heart melt as you gaze at them. When night has almost fallen and the sky is dark over the blackened earth, the sea still faintly gleams, by we know not what mysterious and glowing relic of the day that has sunk beneath the waves.

She refreshes our imagination because she does not make us think of the life of men, but she rejoices our soul, because she is, like our soul, an infinite and powerless aspiration, a forward momentum forever failing, an eternal and gentle lament. She thus enchants us like music, which unlike language does not bear the trace of things, and tells us nothing of men, but mimics the movements of our souls. Our heart as it rushes forward with their waves, and falls back with them, thus forgets its own failings, and takes consolation in an intimate harmony between its sadness and that of the sea, which melds its own destiny with theirs.

– September 1892

Seascape

I have lost the sense of certain words: perhaps I ought to learn it again by listening to all those things which have long opened a path leading inside me, one that has been neglected for many years, but one that can be followed again and which, I firmly believe, is not forever closed. I would need to go back to Normandy, not making any particular effort, but just going to the coast. Or rather I would take the wooded paths from which you occasionally catch sight of it and where the breeze mingles together the smell of the salt, damp leaves and milk. I would ask nothing from all these natal things. They are generous to the child whose birth they witnessed, and they would of their own free will teach him the things he has forgotten. Everything, its odour first of all, would tell me that the sea was near – but I would still not have seen it. I would hear it faintly. I would follow a path of hawthorns, once so familiar to me, with tender emotion, and with anxiety too at the prospect of suddenly spotting, through a gap in the hedge, the invisible, ever-present friend, the madwoman at her eternal laments, the old melancholy queen, the sea. Suddenly I would see her; it would be on one of those days of somnolence beneath a dazzling sun, when she reflects the sky that is as blue as she is, only paler. Sails white like butterflies would be dotted over the motionless water, happy not to move any more, almost swooning in the heat. Or alternatively, the sea would be rough, yellow in the sunlight like a great field of mud, with swells that, from such a distance, would appear stationary and crowned with dazzling snow.

Sails in harbour

In the harbour, narrow and long like a watery highway between its low quays along which gleamed the lights of evening, passers-by stopped to gaze at the vessels that had assembled there like noble strangers who had arrived the day before and were ready to set off once more. These ships, indifferent to the curiosity they aroused amongst a crowd whose vulgarity they seemed to disdain or whose language, quite simply, they did not speak, preserved, in the liquid lodgings where they had stopped for the night, their silent and immobile momentum. Their strong stems spoke no less eloquently of the long journeys they still had to accomplish than the signs of wear and tear on them spoke of the fatigues they had already withstood on those gliding roads, as ancient as the world and as new as the passage that cuts them and which they do not outlive. Frail and resistant, they were turned with a sad pride towards the Ocean which they dominate and in which they seemed so lost. The marvellous and skilful intricacy of the rigging was reflected in the water like an exact and farsighted intelligence plunging headlong into the uncertain destiny which sooner or later will break it. So recently withdrawn from the terrible and splendid life in which they would again be immersed the very next day, their sails still drooped from the wind that had made them belly out, their bowsprits bent out over the water just as they themselves had done so only yesterday, impelled by their forward momentum; and, from stem to stern, the curve of their hulls seemed to preserve the mysterious and flexible grace of their wake.

1

> *'Give us good things, whether we ask for them or not, and keep away from us evil things, even if we ask you for them.'* – *This prayer seems right and effective. If you find anything in it that needs correcting, don't keep it to yourself.*
> (Plato)

'My little tree, my little donkey, my mother, my brother, my country, my God, my little stranger, my little lotus, my little sea shell, my darling, my little plant, go away, let me get dressed and I'll see you in the rue de la Baume at eight o'clock. Please don't arrive after a quarter past eight, because I'm starving.'

She tried to close the door of her bedroom on Honoré, but he added, 'Neck!', and she proffered her neck with a docility and an exaggerated zeal that made him burst out laughing.

'Even if you didn't want to,' he told her, 'there exist between your neck and my mouth, between your ears and my moustache, between your hands and my hands, close relations of friendship. I'm sure that these relations would not cease if we no longer loved one another, any more than, even since I've quarrelled with my cousin Pauline, I can stop my footman going every evening to chat to her chambermaid. It's of its own free will and without my assent that my mouth moves towards your neck.'

They were now just a step away from one another. Suddenly their eyes met and each of them tried to fix in the eyes of the other the thought that they were in love; she remained for a second thus, standing erect, before collapsing breathless onto a chair, as if she had been running. And they said to each other, at almost the same time, with intense exaltation, uttering the words deliberately with their lips, as if preparing to kiss:

'My love!'

She repeated in a sad and mournful tone, as she shook her head:

'Yes, my love.'

She knew he could not resist this little head movement; he threw himself on her and kissed her and said to her slowly, 'Naughty girl!', so tenderly that her eyes grew moist.

The clock chimed half past seven. He left.

On his return home, Honoré kept repeating to himself, 'My mother, my brother, my country' – he stopped – 'yes, my country!… my little sea shell, my little tree,' and he could not restrain a laugh as he uttered these words that they had so quickly adopted for their own ends, those little words that can seem empty and that they had filled with infinite meaning. Trusting unthinkingly in the fertile and inventive genius of their love, they had little by little seen it endow them with a language of their own, as if they were an entire nation to be given weapons, games and laws.

As he dressed for dinner, his thought hung effortlessly on the moment when he would see her again, just as a gymnast already touches the still distant trapeze towards which he is flying, or just as a musical phrase seems to reach the chord that will resolve it and is already pulling it towards itself, by virtue of the very distance between them, with all the strength of the desire that promises that phrase and summons it into being. Thus it was that Honoré had over the past year been wishing his life away, hurrying forward, as soon as it was morning, to the time in the afternoon when he would see her. And his days in reality were not composed of twelve or fourteen different hours, but of the four or five half-hours that he longed for and then looked back on.

Honoré had already been at the home of the Princesse d'Alériouvre for a few minutes, when Mme Seaune came in. She greeted her hostess and the different guests, and seemed less to wish Honoré a good evening than to take his hand as she might have done in the middle of a conversation. If their relationship had been public knowledge, it might have seemed as if they had arrived together, and that she had waited for a few moments outside the door so as not to come in at the same time as him. But even if they had not seen each other for two days (which over the last year had not happened a single time), they would still not have experienced that joyful surprise at being reunited which lies behind every friendly hello, since, unable to go five minutes without thinking of each other, they could never actually meet again, since they never separated.

During the dinner, each time they spoke to each other, their manners surpassed in vivacity and gentleness those of a mere pair of friends, but were imbued with a majestic and natural respect that is unknown among lovers. They thus appeared similar to those gods who, according to fable, lived in disguise among men, or like two angels whose fraternal familiarity exalts the joy, but does not diminish the respect that is inspired in them by the shared nobility of their origins and their mysterious blood. At the same time as it yielded to the powerful scent of the irises and roses that reigned languidly on the table, the air was gradually imbued with the perfume of the tenderness that Honoré and Françoise naturally emitted. At certain moments, it seemed to spread its fragrance with a violence even more delicious than its habitual gentleness, a violence that nature had not allowed them to moderate any more than it has allowed a heliotrope in the sun to do so, or lilacs blooming in the rain.

Thus it was that their tenderness, not being secret, was all the more mysterious. Everyone could approach it, just as everyone can approach those impenetrable and defenceless bracelets on the wrists of a woman in love, which bear written in unknown and visible characters the name that gives life or death, whose meaning they seem ceaselessly to offer to the curious and disappointed eyes that cannot grasp it.

'How much longer will I continue to love her?' Honoré asked himself as he rose from table. He recalled how many passions, which at their birth he had thought immortal, had in fact lasted only a short time, and the certainty that this passion would one day end cast a shadow over his tenderness.

Then he remembered how, that very morning, while he was at mass, as the priest was reading the Gospel and saying, 'Jesus, stretching out his hand, told them: That creature is my brother, and my mother also and all my family,' he had for a moment held out his entire soul to God, trembling but erect, like a palm tree, and had prayed, 'My God! My God! Give me the grace to love her forever. My God, this is the only grace I ask of you, grant me, my God, you who can ensure it, grant me that I may love her forever!'

Now, in one of those altogether physical hours when the soul effaces itself within us behind the stomach busy digesting, behind the skin which is still rejoicing in its recent ablution and its clean underwear, and the mouth that enjoys a smoke, and the eye which feasts on naked shoulders and gleaming lights, he repeated his prayer with less intensity, doubtful that a miracle would come to disturb the psychological law of his inconstancy, a law as impossible to break as the physical laws of gravity or death.

She saw his preoccupied eyes, rose, and coming up to him (he hadn't seen her), as they were quite some distance away from the others, she said to him in that drawling, whimpering tone of voice, the tone of a small child which always made him laugh, and as if he had just spoken to her:

'What?'

He started to laugh and told her:

'Don't say another word, or I'll kiss you, d'you hear, I'll kiss you in front of everybody!'

She started to laugh, then, assuming her sad and discontented voice again, to amuse him, she said:

'Yes, yes, that's just fine, you weren't thinking of me in the slightest!'

And he, gazing at her and laughing, replied:

'How easily you tell lies!' and, gently, he added, 'You naughty, naughty girl!'

She left him and went over to talk to the others. Honoré reflected, 'when I feel my heart growing detached from her, I'll try to withdraw it so gently that she won't feel a thing. I will still be just as tender, just as respectful. I will conceal from her the new love which will have replaced my love for her in my heart just as carefully as I conceal from her right now the pleasures which my body enjoys here and there without her and separate from her.' (He glanced towards the Princess d'Alériouvre.) And for her part, he would let her gradually settle her affections elsewhere, and start a new life. He would not be jealous, and would even point out the men who would seem to him to offer her a more decent or a more glorious homage. The more he imagined Françoise as another woman whom he did not love, but all of whose charm and wit he appreciated as a connoisseur, the more did sharing her seem the noble and easy thing to do. The words 'tolerant and warm friendship', and 'a fine act of charity performed for the worthiest of recipients, giving them the best thing one has', came and hovered on his slack, serene lips.

Just then, Françoise, seeing that it was ten o'clock, bade everyone goodnight and left. Honoré accompanied her to her carriage, imprudently kissed her in the darkness, and came back in.

Three hours later, Honoré was walking home with M. de Buivres, whose return from Tonkin had been celebrated that evening.[13] Honoré was asking him about the Princesse d'Alériouvre who, having been left a widow at more or less same age as Françoise, was much more beautiful than her. Honoré, without being in love with her, would have greatly enjoyed the pleasure of possessing her if he could have been certain of doing so without Françoise finding out and being hurt.

'Nobody knows much about her,' said M. de Buivres, 'or at least nobody knew much when I went away – I haven't seen anybody since I got back.'

'In short, there weren't any easy pickings, this evening,' concluded Honoré.

'No, not much,' replied M. de Buivres; and as Honoré had reached his door, the conversation was about to end when M. de Buivres added:

'Except for Madame Seaune to whom you must have been introduced, since you were there at dinner. If you fancy her, it can easily be arranged. But she wouldn't tell *me* as much!'

'I've never heard anyone say what you've just told me,' said Honoré.

'You're young,' said M. de Buivres, 'and anyway, this evening there was someone there who had a bit of a fling with her, I think that's beyond dispute: that young chap François de Gouvres. He says she's pretty hot-blooded! But it appears she hasn't got much of a figure. He decided he didn't want to continue. I bet that, as we're speaking, she's living it up somewhere or other. Did you notice how she always leaves social gatherings early?'

'But ever since she's been widowed, she's lived in the same house as her brother, and she wouldn't risk the concierge telling everyone she comes back in the middle of the night.'

'But my dear boy, between ten o'clock and one in the morning, there's plenty of time to get up to all sorts of things! And then, who knows? But it'll be one o'clock in no time, you really ought to toddle off to bed.'

He himself rang the door-bell; after a short while, the door opened; Buivres held out his hand to Honoré, who bade him a mechanical farewell, went in, suddenly felt possessed by an insane need to go out again, but found the door had closed heavily behind him; and apart from his candle waiting for him, burning impatiently at the foot of the stairs, there was no other light. He did not dare awaken the concierge to open the door for him, and he went up to his room.

2

Our acts our angels are, or good or ill,
Our fatal shadows that walk by us still.
(Beaumont and Fletcher)

Life had changed considerably for Honoré ever since the day when M. de Buivres had, among so many others, made certain remarks to him – remarks similar to those which Honoré himself had listened to or uttered so many times with complete indifference – but which he could no longer get out of his head, either during the daytime when he was alone, or through the long night. He had immediately asked Françoise a few questions: she loved him too much and suffered too much at his pain to dream of taking offence; she had sworn to him that she had never deceived him and never would deceive him.

When he was with her, when he was holding her little hands and saying to them, quoting Verlaine's line:

Oh lovely little hands that will close my eyes,

when he heard her saying to him, 'My brother, my country, my beloved,' and her voice aroused prolonged echoes in his heart with all the sweetness of the church bells in one's place of birth, he believed her; and even though he did not feel quite as happy as he had before, at least it did not seem to him impossible that his convalescent heart might one day rediscover happiness. But when he was far away from Françoise, and even sometimes when he was near her and noticed her eyes gleaming with a fire that he immediately imagined had been kindled elsewhere – who knows, yesterday, perhaps, and again the day after – kindled by another man; when, having yielded to the purely physical desire for another woman, and recalling how many times he had so yielded and managed to lie about it to Françoise without ceasing to love her, he no longer found it absurd to suppose that she too was lying to him, that it was not even necessary for her not to love him if she were to lie to him, and that before knowing him she had thrown herself on other men with the same ardour that now consumed him – an ardour that appeared to him more terrible than the ardour that he inspired in her appeared sweet, since he saw it with the eyes of imagination that magnifies everything.

Then, he tried to tell her that he had deceived her; he made this experiment not out of vengeance or any need to make her suffer in the same way that he did, but so that she would reciprocate by telling him the truth as well, and above all so that he would no longer sense the lie within him, and to expiate the misdeeds of his sensuality, since in order to create an object for his jealousy it seemed to him at times that it was his own lie and his own sensuality that he was projecting onto Françoise.

It was one evening, as he was taking a walk along the avenue des Champs-Elysées, that he tried to tell her that he had deceived her. He was alarmed to see her grow pale and sit down suddenly on a bench, overcome; and all the more alarmed when she pushed away, without anger and even with gentleness, in her sincere and heart-stricken despondency, the hand he was stretching out towards her. For two days, he thought he had lost her or rather that he had found her again. But this involuntary, spectacular and melancholy proof of love that she had just given him was not enough for Honoré. Even if he had gained the impossible certainty that she had only ever belonged to him, the unprecedented suffering that his heart had first experienced on the night when M. de Buivres had taken him back to his house – not a similar suffering, or the memory of that suffering, but that very same suffering – would never have ceased to afflict him, even if it could have been demonstrated to him that it was without foundation. Thus it is that we still tremble on awakening at the memory of the murderer whom we have already recognised to be the illusion caused by a dream; thus it is that amputees suffer throughout their lives in the leg that they have lost.

In vain he had spent the day walking, worn himself out on horseback, on his bicycle, fencing; in vain he had met Françoise, taken her back to her home, and, in the evening, gathered from her hands, her forehead and her eyes the trust and peace, as sweet as honey, with which he returned home, calmed and enriched with their sweet-smelling store; hardly was he back home than he started to worry, slipped quickly into bed so as to get off to sleep before anything happened to his happiness that, carefully embalmed in that fresh and recent tenderness only one hour old would travel through the night until the next day, intact and glorious like a prince of Egypt; but it seemed that Buivres's words, or one of the innumerable images he had since formed in his thoughts, were on the point of appearing to his mind's eye, and then there would be no prospect of sleep. That image had still not appeared, but he sensed it lying in wait and, stiffening his resolve against it, he would re-light his candle, read, and endeavour to cram his brain mercilessly full of the meaning of the sentences he was reading, not leaving a single gap, so as to prevent that dread image from having a single moment or the tiniest little place to slip in.

But all at once, there it was: it had managed to get in, and now he could not get it out again; the door of his attention that he had been holding shut with all his might, exhausting himself in the effort, had been forced open; then it had shut again, and he was going to have to spend the night with this horrible companion. So there was no doubt about it, it was definite, this night like all the others he would not get a minute's sleep; so off he went to get the bottle of Bromidia, swallowed three spoonfuls and, certain now that he would be able to sleep, and even alarmed at the thought that he would not be able to do anything *but* sleep, whatever happened, he started to think about Françoise again, with panic, with despair, with hatred. He wanted to take advantage of the fact that his affair with her was not common knowledge to make bets on her virtue with other men, to throw them at her, to see if she would yield, to try to discover something, to find out everything, to hide in a bedroom (he remembered doing so for fun when he was younger) and see it all. He would not hesitate at the thought of the other men, since he would have asked them to do it seemingly as a joke – otherwise, think of the scandal and the uproar! – but in particular because of her, to see if the next day when he asked her, 'You've never deceived me?' she would reply, 'Never,' with that same loving expression. Perhaps she would confess everything, and indeed would have yielded only as a result of his stratagems. And then it would have been the salutary operation after which his love would be cured of the malady that was killing him, just as the malady caused by a parasite kills the tree (he only needed to look at himself in the mirror, lit feebly as it was by his night-time candle, to be sure). But no – the image would always come back, and he did not even try to work out how much stronger it would be than the images formed by his imagination, and with what incalculable power it would strike down on his poor head.

Then, suddenly, he thought of her, her gentleness, her tenderness, her purity, and he felt like weeping at the outrage that for a second he had dreamt of inflicting on her. Just think: the very idea of suggesting it to his party friends!

Soon he sensed the general tremor and feeling of faintness that occurs a few minutes before Bromidia sends you to sleep. Suddenly, aware of nothing, not even a dream or a sensation, occurring between his last thought and his present reflections, he said to himself, 'What, haven't I been asleep yet?' But on seeing that it was broad daylight, he realised that for over six hours, the sleep of Bromidia had possessed him without him actually enjoying it.

He waited for the restless movements in his head to calm down a little, then got up and tried in vain, with the help of cold water and walking up and down, to bring back some of the usual colour to his pale figure and his drawn and weary eyes, so that Françoise would not find him too ugly. On leaving home, he went to church and there, bent and tired, with all the last desperate strength of his broken body that wanted to stand up and grow young again, of his sick and ageing heart that wanted to get better, of his mind, mercilessly harassed and panting and longing for peace, he prayed to God – God to whom, barely two months earlier, he had asked for the grace to love Françoise forever – he now prayed to this God with the same strength, the same strength of that love which in bygone days, sure it was going to die, had asked to live, and which now, frightened at having to live, begged for death – prayed to God to give him the grace *not* to love Françoise any more, not to love her for much longer, not to love her forever, to ensure that he might at last imagine her in the arms of another man without suffering, since he could no longer imagine her except in the arms of another man. And perhaps he would no longer imagine her thus when he could imagine her without suffering.

Then he remembered how often he had been afraid he would not love her forever, how deeply he had engraved in his memory, so that nothing would ever efface them from it, her cheeks always proffered to his lips, her forehead, her little hands, her grave eyes, her adored features. And suddenly, realising they were awoken from their oh-so-sweet calm by the desire for another man, he tried not to think about them and saw all the more obstinately her proffered cheeks, her forehead, her little hands – oh! her little hands! those too! – her grave eyes, her detested features.

From this day onwards, at first horrified at the thought of entering on such a path, he never left Françoise, kept a close eye on her everyday life, accompanied her when she went out paying visits, following her when she went shopping, waiting a whole hour at shop doors for her. If he had been able to imagine that he was thus preventing her from deceiving him in the material sense, he would doubtless have abandoned the attempt, afraid lest she view him with horror; but she allowed him to do all this with so much joy at being able to have him near her the whole time that this joy little by little spread to him, and slowly filled him with a trust and certainty that no material proof could have given him, like those people in prey to a hallucination who are sometimes cured by making them touch the armchair or the living person occupying the place which they thought was occupied by a phantom, and thus chasing the phantom away from the real world by virtue of the very reality that will no longer afford it any room.

In this way Honoré, by shedding light on all of Françoise's daytime activities and mentally filling them with definite occupations, managed to suppress those gaps and those shadows in which the evil spirits of jealousy and doubt that assailed him every evening came to lie in ambush. He could sleep again, his sufferings were more infrequent and shorter, and if he then summoned her over, a few moments of her presence could calm him down for an entire night.

3

> *The soul can be trusted to the end. That which is so beautiful and attractive as these relations must be succeeded and supplanted only by what is more beautiful, and so on forever.*
> (Emerson)

The salon of Madame Seaune, née the Princess of Galaise-Orlandes, of whom we have spoken in the first part of this narrative under her first name, Françoise, is even today one of the most sought-after salons in Paris. In a society where the title of Duchess would not have set her apart from a host of other women, her bourgeois name is as distinctive as a beauty spot on a face, and in exchange for the title she lost when she married M. Seaune, she has acquired the prestige of having voluntarily renounced such a lofty glory for a well-born imagination, white peacocks, black swans, white violets and captive queens.

Mme Seaune has held many receptions this year and last year, but her salon was closed for the three preceding years – those which followed the death of Honoré de Tenvres.

The friends of Honoré, who had rejoiced to see him little by little recover his erstwhile healthy looks and his gaiety, now constantly met him in the company of Madame Seaune and attributed his new lease of life to this relationship that they imagined to be a recent development.

It was barely two months after Honoré's complete recovery that there occurred the accident in the avenue in the Bois de Boulogne, in which he had both his legs broken under a runaway horse.

The accident happened on the first Tuesday in May; peritonitis set in on the Sunday. Honoré received the sacraments on Monday and passed away on the same Monday at six o'clock in the evening. But from the Tuesday, the day of the accident, to the Sunday evening, he was the only one to think that he was dying.

On the Tuesday, at around six o'clock, after his wounds had first been dressed, he asked to be left alone, but requested that he be shown the calling cards of the people who had already come to enquire how he was.

That very morning, more than eight hours previously, he had been walking down the avenue of the Bois de Boulogne. He had breathed his joy in and out, in the air with its fresh breeze and its sunlight, he had recognised that joy deep in the eyes of the women who admiringly followed his rapid handsome figure, momentarily lost sight of it as his capricious gaiety took another turn, then effortlessly regained it as the galloping and steaming horses overtook it, and tasted it in his youthful and avid mouth watering in the sweet air – the same profound joy that made life so beautiful that morning, the life of the sun, the shade, the sky, the stones, the easterly wind and the trees, trees as majestic as men standing erect, and as restful as women asleep in their glittering immobility.

One moment, he had looked to see what time it was, retraced his steps, and then… then it had happened. In a second, the horse that he had not even seen had broken both his legs. It did not seem to him in the slightest that this second needed to have turned out necessarily the way it did. At that same second he could easily have been a little further on, or a little less far, or the horse could have been diverted from its course, or, if it had been raining, he would have gone home, or, if he had not looked to see what time it was, he would not have retraced his steps and would have carried on as far as the waterfall. And yet, the thing that might just as well not have happened (so much so that he could pretend for a moment that it was merely a dream) was something real, and was now part of his life, without him being able to change a thing about it by mere force of will. He had two broken legs and a bruised stomach. Oh, the accident in itself was not so very extraordinary; he remembered that, not a week ago, during dinner at the home of Dr S***, they had been talking about C***, who had been wounded in the same way by a runaway horse. When they asked how the patient was doing, the Doctor had replied, 'He's in a bad way.' Honoré had persisted, asked questions about the wound, and the Doctor had replied, in a self-important, pedantic and melancholy tone of voice, 'But it's not just the wound; you have to look at the whole picture; his sons are a worry to him; he doesn't have the same high position he used to have; the attacks of newspapers have dealt him quite a blow. I only wish I was wrong, but he's in a damn awful state.' Having said those words, as the Doctor felt that *he*, on the contrary, was in an excellent state, healthier, cleverer and more admired than ever, as Honoré knew that Françoise loved him more and more deeply, that the world had accepted their relationship and bowed down no less to their happiness than to the greatness of character of Françoise; and as finally the wife of Dr S***, shaken at the thought of the wretched end and the loneliness of C***, forbade, as a measure of hygiene, both herself and her children from thinking of sad events or even going to funerals, everyone repeated one last time, 'Poor old C***, he's in a bad way' while swallowing a last glass of champagne and sensing, from the pleasure they derived from drinking it, that '*they* were in an excellent way'.

But this was not at all the same thing. Honoré now felt submerged by the thought of his unhappy fate, as he had often been by that of the fate of others, but now he could no longer find any firm footing within himself. He felt the ground of good health slipping away from under his feet – that ground on which grow our highest resolutions and our most graceful joys, just as oaks and violets have their roots in the black damp earth; and at each step he took within himself, he stumbled. When the Doctor had been talking about C*** at that dinner he was now remembering, he had said, 'Already before his accident, ever since the newspapers had started attacking him, I'd met C*** and thought how sallow he looked, with hollow eyes and a really lousy appearance!' And the Doctor had drawn his hand, so celebrated for its skill and beauty, across his full, pink face, through his long, fine, well-kept beard, and everyone had taken pleasure in imagining their own healthy appearance in the same way that a property owner dwells with satisfaction on the sight of his tenant, still young, tranquil and rich. Now when Honoré looked at himself in the mirror he was alarmed at his 'sallow face' and his 'lousy appearance'. And immediately the thought that the Doctor would say for him the same words as for C***, with the same indifference, terrified him. The very same people who would come to him full of pity would turn away quickly enough, as if from an object that was dangerous for them; they would end up obeying the protests of their own good health, their desire for happiness and life. Then his thoughts returned to Françoise and, his shoulders bent, and his head drooping in spite of itself, as if God's commandment had been hovering there over him, he realised with a boundless and submissive sadness that he would have to renounce her. He felt the sensation of the humility of his body, bowing down in childlike weakness, with all the resignation of a patient, under that immense sorrow, and he felt pity for himself just as, across the intervening distance of his whole life, he had often seen himself as still a small child who aroused his own sympathy, and he felt like weeping.

He heard a knock at the door. The calling cards he had requested were brought in. He knew full well that people would come for news of him, since he was quite aware that his accident was serious, but even so he had not expected there to be so many cards, and he was alarmed to see that so many people had come, people who did not know him well and who would have made the effort only if he was to be married or buried. There was a whole heap of cards and the concierge was carrying it carefully so it would not fall off the big tray: the cards were practically overflowing. But all of a sudden, once he had these cards all next to him, the heap appeared such a little thing, really quite ridiculously little, much littler than the chair or the fireplace. And he was even more alarmed that it was so little, and he felt so alone that to distract himself he started feverishly to read the names; one card, two cards, three cards, ah! He shuddered, and looked closer: 'Count François de Gouvres'. And yet he might well have expected M. de Gouvres to come and enquire after him, but he had not thought of him for a long while, and suddenly the words of Buivres came back to him: *'this evening there was someone there who's had a bit of a fling with her: François de Gouvres; he says she's pretty hot-blooded; but it appears she hasn't got much of a figure, and he decided he didn't want to continue'*, and experiencing all the old suffering rising momentarily from the depths of his consciousness to the surface, he said to himself, 'Now I'm only too glad if I *am* dying. Imagine not dying, being stuck in this situation, maybe for years, and her not with me for part of the day and all of the night – seeing her at another man's! And now it wouldn't be my sickly imagination causing me to see her like that, it would be a certain fact. How could she still love me? An amputee!' Suddenly he stopped. 'And if I die, after me?'

She was thirty; in a single bound he leapt over the shorter or longer time she would remember him and remain faithful. But a time would come… 'He says *she's pretty hot-blooded*… I want to love, I want to live and I want to be able to walk, I want to follow her everywhere, I want to be handsome, I want her to love me!'

Just then, he felt afraid; he could hear his wheezy breath; his side hurt, his chest seemed to have caved in to meet his back, he could not breathe the way he wanted, he tried to draw breath but could not. At every second he felt himself breathing and yet not breathing enough. The doctor came. Honoré was simply suffering an attack of nervous asthma. Once the doctor had gone, he felt even sadder; he would have preferred it to be more serious so he could arouse pity. For he felt that even if *this* was not serious, something else was, and he was slipping away. Now he recalled all the physical sufferings in his life, and was filled with sorrow; those who had most loved him had never pitied him on the pretext that he suffered from nervous disorders. In the terrible months he had spent after his return home with Buivres, when at seven o'clock he got dressed after walking all through the night, his brother, who would wake up for a quarter of an hour on the nights following over-copious dinners, would tell him:

'You pay too much attention to yourself; there are nights when I can't sleep either. Anyway, people think they can't sleep a wink when in fact they always manage to doze off for a bit.'

It was true that he paid himself too much attention; in the background to his life he could always hear death, which had never left him entirely and which, without altogether destroying his life, kept undermining it, now in one place, now in another. Now his asthma was getting worse, he could not draw breath, his whole chest made a painful effort to breathe in. And he sensed the veil which hides life from us, the death which dwells within us, being drawn apart, and he realised what a terrifying thing it is to breathe, to live.

Then, he found himself carried forward to the time when she would have found consolation, and then – which man would it be? And his jealousy panicked at the uncertainty of the event and its necessity. He could have prevented it while still living, but he could not live, and so?... She would say she was going to enter a convent, then once he was dead she would have second thoughts. No! He preferred not to be deceived twice over: better to know. – Who? – Gouvres, Alériouvre, Buivres, Breyves? He could see them all and, teeth clenched tight together, he felt the furious rebellion that at that moment was doubtless twisting his face into an indignant grimace. He managed to calm down. 'No,' he thought, 'it won't be that, not a libertine – it must be a man who truly loves her. Why don't I want it to be some libertine? I'm crazy to ask myself the question, it's so natural. Because I love her for herself, and want her to be happy. – No, it's not that, I don't want anyone to arouse her senses, to give her more pleasure than I have given her, or even to give her any pleasure at all. I want someone to give her happiness, or to give her love, but I don't want anyone to give her pleasure. I am jealous of the other's pleasure, and of her pleasure. I won't be jealous of their love. She must get married, she must choose wisely... Even so, it will be sad.'

Then one of the desires he had had as a small child came back to him – the small child he had been at the age of seven, when he went to bed every evening at eight o'clock. When his mother, instead of staying until midnight in her bedroom which was next to Honoré's, and then going to bed there, had arranged to go out at eleven and passed the time until then getting dressed, he would beg her to get dressed before dinner and to go away somewhere, anywhere, since he could not stand the idea that, while he was trying to go to sleep, people in his home were getting ready to go out for the evening. And so as to give him pleasure and calm him down, his mother, in the finery of her low-cut evening dress, would come in at eight o'clock to say goodnight before going off to the home of a lady friend to wait until it was time for the ball. And this was the only way on which, on those days – so sad for him – when his mother went to the ball, he could, sorrowful but tranquil, get off to sleep.

Now, the same prayer that he had addressed to his mother rose to his lips, addressed in turn to Françoise. He would like to have asked her to get married straight away, to be all ready and waiting, so that he could finally get off to sleep forever, heavy at heart but calm and not in the least worried by what would happen after he had gone to sleep.

The following days, he tried to speak to Françoise who, like the doctor himself, did not think he was dying and refused, with a gentle but inflexible firmness, to agree to Honoré's request.

They were so much in the habit of telling each other the truth that each of them even told truths that might hurt the other, as if deep down in both of them, in their highly strung and sensitive nature, whose susceptibilities they had to treat with kid gloves, they had sensed the presence of a God, superior and indifferent to all these precautions that are fit only for children; a God who demanded the truth and owed the truth to them. And both of them had – Honoré towards this God deep within Françoise, and Françoise towards this God deep within Honoré – always sensed that they had duties before which the desire not to be pained and not to be offended was forced to yield, and the most sincere lies of tenderness and pity had to give way.

So when Françoise told Honoré he was going to live, he felt clearly that she believed what she was saying and he persuaded himself little by little to believe it too.

'If I have to die, I won't be jealous when I'm dead; but what about *until* I'm dead? As long as my body lives, yes! But since it is only the pleasure I'm jealous of, since it's my body which is jealous, since what I'm jealous of isn't her heart, isn't her happiness, which I wish her to have with whoever is most capable of giving it to her; when my body is effaced, when the soul wins out from it, when I am gradually detached from material things as I was one evening when I was really ill, then I won't be consumed by such a mad desire for the body and I will love the soul all the more: I won't be jealous. And then I will truly love. I can't conceive what it will be, now that my body is still full of life and rebelliousness, but I can imagine it to some extent, as at those times when I was holding hands with Françoise, and found in a boundless tenderness, free of desire, an appeasement for my sufferings and my jealousy. I will feel great sorrow on leaving her, but the sorrow will be that which in previous days brought me closer to myself, that which an angel came to console within me, the sorrow which revealed to me the mysterious friend of my days of unhappiness, namely my soul – that calm sorrow, thanks to which I will feel more presentable to God, and not the horrible illness which has caused me such pain for so long without elevating my heart, like a throbbing physical pain which degrades and diminishes us. Together with my body, with the desire for her body, I will be delivered from that. – Yes, but until then, what will become of me? Weaker, more incapable of resisting her than ever, cut down on my two broken legs, when I want to rush over to her to see that she isn't where I dreamt she might be, I'll stay put, unable to move, sniggered at by all those who'll be able to *have a fling with her* as much as they like, in front of me, a sick man whom they will no longer fear.'

On the night of Sunday to Monday, he dreamt he was suffocating, and felt a huge weight on his chest. He begged for mercy, no longer had the strength to shift this great weight; the feeling that it had all been weighing down on him like this for a long, long time was inexplicable to him, he could not tolerate it a second longer, he was choking. Suddenly, he felt himself miraculously relieved of the whole burden which moved further and further away, having delivered him forever. And he said to himself, 'I am dead!'

And, above him, he saw rising up everything that had weighed down for so long on him, suffocating him; he thought at first that it was the image of Gouvres, and then merely his suspicions, then his desires, then that expectant longing that had started as soon as day broke, crying out for the time when he would see Françoise, then the thought of Françoise. At every minute it changed shape, like a cloud, growing bigger, ever bigger, and now he could no longer understand how this thing which he had thought to be as immense as the world had managed to weigh on him, on the little body of a feeble man like himself, on the poor heart of an ailing man like himself, without him being crushed by it. And he also realised that he *had* been crushed and that it had been the life of a crushed man that he had led. And this immense thing that had weighed down on his chest with all the force in the world was, he realised, his love.

Then he repeated to himself, 'the life of a crushed man!' and he remembered that when the horse had knocked him down, he had said to himself, 'I'm going to be crushed'; he remembered his walk, how that morning he had arranged to go and have lunch with Françoise, and then, via that detour, the thought of his love came back to him. And he said to himself, 'Was it my love that was weighing down on me? What could it be if not my love? My character, perhaps? Me? Or else life?' Then he thought, 'No, when I die, I will not be delivered from my love, but from my carnal desires, my carnal longings, my jealousy.' Then he said, 'My God, let that hour come, let it come quickly, my God, let me know perfect love.'

On Sunday evening, peritonitis had set in; on the Monday morning, at around ten, he became feverish, wanted Françoise, called out for her, his eyes burning. 'I want your eyes to shine too, I want to give you pleasure like I've never given you before... I want to give you... so much that it'll hurt you!' Then all of a sudden he went pale with fury. 'I can see perfectly well why you don't want to, I know perfectly well what you had done to you this morning, and where it was and who did it, and I know he wanted someone to come and fetch me and conceal me behind the door so I could see you, without being able to fling myself on you, since I've lost my legs, and wouldn't be able to stop you, since you'd have felt even more pleasure on seeing me there all the way through; he knows so very well everything that needs to be done to give you pleasure, but I'll kill you first, first I'll kill you, and first of all I'll kill myself! See! I *have* killed myself!' And he fell back on the pillow, exhausted.

He gradually calmed down and continued to reflect on who she might marry after his death, but it was always the images he tried to brush away, that of François de Gouvres, that of Buivres, the images that tortured him, that kept coming back.

At midday, he had received the sacraments. The doctor had said he would not last until the evening. He was losing his strength extremely rapidly, could no longer absorb food, had almost lost his hearing. He remained clear-headed and did not speak, so as not to cause pain to Françoise who, he could see, was grief-stricken; he tried to imagine how she would be once he was no more, and he would know nothing of her, and she would no longer be able to love him.

The names he had said mechanically, that very morning, the names of those who would perhaps possess her, started again to stream through his head while his eyes followed a fly that was approaching his finger as if it wanted to touch him, then flew off and kept coming back, though without actually touching him; and when, arousing his attention again after it had drifted off for a while, the name of François de Gouvres came back, and he said that, yes, perhaps he would possess her, while thinking at the same time, 'Perhaps the fly is going to touch the sheet? No, not yet,' he suddenly came out of his reverie and thought, 'What? The one thing doesn't seem to me any more important than the other! Will Gouvres possess Françoise? Will the fly touch the sheet? Oh, possessing Françoise is rather more important.' But the precision with which he could see the difference separating these two events showed him that neither of them particularly touched him more than did the other. And he said to himself, 'So – they are both matters of such indifference? How sad!' Then he realised that he was only saying 'How sad' out of habit, and that having completely changed, he was no longer sad to have changed. A vague smile parted his clenched lips. 'There it is,' he reflected, 'my pure love for Françoise. I'm not jealous, so I must be very close to death; but it hardly matters – it was necessary for me to feel true love for Françoise at last.'

But then, looking up, he saw Françoise, in the midst of the servants, the doctor, and his two elderly women relatives, who were all there, praying right nearby. And he realised how that love, pure of all egotism and all sensuality – the love he wanted to be so gentle, so vast and so divine within him – cherished the elderly relatives, the servants and the doctor himself as much as it did Françoise, and that since he already felt for her the love of all creatures to which his soul, similar to theirs, now united him, he had no other love for her. He could not even imagine feeling any pain at this, so much was any exclusive love for her, and even the idea of any preference for her, now abolished.

In tears, at the foot of the bed, she was murmuring the most beautiful words of days gone by: 'My country, my brother.' But he, having neither the desire nor the strength to undeceive her, smiled and reflected that his 'country' was no longer in her, but in heaven and over all the earth. He repeated in his heart, 'my brothers,' and if he gazed at her more than at the others, it was simply out of pity, for the flood of tears that he could see flowing right under his eyes, his eyes that would soon close and already had stopped weeping. But he did not love her any more or any differently than he loved the doctor, or his elderly relatives, or the servants. And *that* was the end of his jealousy.

1. 'Vigée' refers to the artist Elisabeth Vigée-Lebrun (1755–1842). The first, de luxe edition of *Pleasures and Days* was embellished with watercolours by Madeleine Lemaire, acknowledged by Proust a few lines earlier.

2. Bouillet, a nineteenth-century French historian, wrote among other things a *Dictionnaire universel d'histoire et de géographie* (1842); the other works mentioned (such as the *Almanach de Gotha*) were all guides to aristocratic society.

3. In Flaubert's last unfinished novel, the eponymous heroes Bouvard and Pécuchet come into some money and retire to the countryside where they proceed to devote themselves, in a series of grimly farcical episodes, to cultivating the arts and sciences of their age: en route, they run through most of the clichéd opinions their society has to offer. Proust here mimics Flaubert both stylistically and thematically.

4. *Domino noir* (1837) was a comic opera by Daniel-François-Esprit Auber (1782–1871) and Eugène Scribe (1791–1861).

5. Charles Lamoureux was a conductor who founded the 'Concerts Lamoureux'; Jules-Edouard Colonne was also a conductor who promoted the work of Berlioz and Wagner.

6. This is a quotation from Racine's *Phèdre* (1677), spoken by its lovelorn protagonist Phaedra.

7. From Wagner's *Meistersinger*: 'The beak of the bird who sang today has become lovely.'

8. Theocritus (d. *c*.250 BC) is best known for his Sicilian *Idylls*.

9. Most of these painters and musicians are well-known: the presence of the 'Golden Age' figures of Cuyp and Potter among the former attests to Proust's love of Dutch landscape painting.

10. A quotation from Victor Hugo's Romantic play *Hernani* (1830).

11. Jacques François Fromental Elie Halévy (1799–1862) and Henri Meilhac (1831–1897) are perhaps best known now as the librettists of Bizet's *Carmen*.

12. François de Curel (d. 1928) was a playwright.

13. Tonkin (or Tongking), the area corresponding to southern Vietnam, was a French protectorate from 1884.

SELECTED TITLES FROM HESPERUS PRESS

Author	Title	Foreword writer
Pietro Aretino	*The School of Whoredom*	Paul Bailey
Honoré de Balzac	*Colonel Chabert*	A.N. Wilson
Charles Baudelaire	*On Wine and Hashish*	Margaret Drabble
Mikhail Bulgakov	*The Fatal Eggs*	Doris Lessing
Giacomo Casanova	*The Duel*	Tim Parks
Miguel de Cervantes	*The Dialogue of the Dogs*	Ben Okri
Anton Chekhov	*Three Years*	William Fiennes
Marquis de Sade	*Incest*	Janet Street-Porter
Fyodor Dostoevsky	*The Double*	Jeremy Dyson
Gustave Flaubert	*Memoirs of a Madman*	Germaine Greer
Giuseppe Garibaldi	*My Life*	Tim Parks
Théophile Gautier	*The Jinx*	Gilbert Adair
André Gide	*Theseus*	
Victor Hugo	*The Last Day of a Condemned Man*	Libby Purves
Joris-Karl Huysmans	*With the Flow*	Simon Callow
Franz Kafka	*Metamorphosis*	Martin Jarvis
Leonardo da Vinci	*Prophecies*	Eraldo Affinati
Nikolai Leskov	*Lady Macbeth of Mtsensk*	Gilbert Adair
Guy de Maupassant	*Butterball*	Germaine Greer
Lorenzino de' Medici	*Apology for a Murder*	Tim Parks
Antoine François Prévost	*Manon Lescaut*	Germaine Greer
Alexander Pushkin	*Dubrovsky*	Patrick Neate
François Rabelais	*Gargantua*	Paul Bailey
François Rabelais	*Pantagruel*	Paul Bailey
Stendhal	*Memoirs of an Egotist*	Doris Lessing
Ivan Turgenev	*Faust*	Simon Callow
Emile Zola	*For a Night of Love*	A.N. Wilson

Marcel Proust was born in Paris to bourgeois parents, in July 1871. His mother came from a well-off Jewish family, and his father was a doctor. In the 1890s, Proust began to move in fashionable Parisian circles, frequenting salons such as that of Mme Arman, a friend of Anatole France. Under the patronage of Anatole France, he published his first book, *Les Plaisirs et les Jours [Pleasures and Days]* in 1896. After this, Proust devoted several years to translating and annotating the works of the art historian John Ruskin. He published a number of articles on Ruskin, as well as two translations: *The Bible of Amiens* in 1904 and *Sesame and Lilies* in 1906. In February of 1907, he published an article in *Le Figaro* entitled '*Sentiments filiaux d'un parricide*', in which he analysed two elements which would become fundamental to his future psychological approach to literature: memory and guilt. Early in 1908, Proust wrote a series of pastiches for *Le Figaro* entitled *Pastiches et mélanges*, in which he imitated the style of Balzac, Flaubert, Sainte-Beuve and other prose writers of the nineteenth century. During the summer of 1909, he began to develop an essay entitled '*Contre Sainte-Beuve*' into a novel which he would continue to write for the rest of his life. In May of 1913 he entitled it *À la recherche du temps perdu [In Search of Lost Time]*.

The first part, *Du Côté de chez Swann*, was published in November 1913. The second part, *À l'ombre des jeunes filles en fleurs*, was delayed by the War until June 1919, but it won the Prix Goncourt in December of that year. Proust continued working on the novel for the last three years of his life, and during this time, three more volumes appeared: *Le côté de Guermantes I* (October 1920), *Le côté de Guermantes II – Sodome et Gomorrhe I* (May 1921), *Sodome et Gomorrhe II* (April 1922).

Proust died of pneumonia on 18th November 1922. The remaining volumes of his novel were published posthumously. They were *La Prisonnière* (1923), *Albertine disparue* (1925) and *Le Temps retrouvé* (1927).